Praise for *The Secret Heiress*

Reveiwers have said….

"It's a great read, full of steamy scenes and situations, witty dialogues and good secondary characters, and some twists and turns. The Secret Heiress will awake butterflies on your tummy." –Romorror Fan Girl

"I thought the author did a wonderful job with Anna's character…This is a great read! " –Harps Book Review

"I just couldn't get enough of this beautiful couple and the hurdles they encountered in coming together."

"The plot is strong and well developed, flowing beautifully, there are several twists, witty and great dialogues and lovable and interesting charcters."

"This love story of Anna and Allistair is worthy of Five Stars."

About the Author
Susie Warren writes heartfelt and passionate contemporary romance with tempting, larger than life heroes and smart, sassy heroines. The stories are set in elite and glamorous worlds and appeal to readers looking for an escape from everyday life by offering jet-set lifestyles and sophisticated plots. Her contemporary series, *The Rosa Legacy* and *The Bolles Dynasty*, feature remarkable, stylish women and the sinfully tempting heroes that challenge them to reveal their secrets, their strengths and their deepest emotions. Susie lives in New York with her inventor husband and their two independent teenagers and at times a world-travelling college kid.

Visit her website, **www.susiewarren.com**, to sign up for her newsletter and a chance to read her next book early, receive information on discounted prices and free books!

The Bolles Dynasty Series
Meet the Bolles Family – Billionaire Oliver Bolles died tragically in a motorcycle accident, leaving his family to deal with speculation around his numerous affairs and rumors surrounding his imploding empire. In the years that follow, his legacy is gradually revealed and his adult children are forced to come to terms with new siblings and past indiscretions.
Book 1: The Forgotten Heiress
Book 2: The Secret Heiress
Book 3: The Chosen Heir
Book 4: The Sheltered Heiress
Book 5: The Rebellious Heir
Book 6: The Protected Heiress

The
Secret
Heiress

SUSIE
WARREN

The Bolles Dynasty ◆ Book 2

The Secret Heiress

Copyright 2015 by Susie Warren
Published by Susie Warren
ISBN: 978-0-9903290-9-1

Second Edition – Rewritten and Revised 2016

Cover design by The Killion Group
Formatting by Susie Warren

For more information on the author and her works, please see www.SusieWarren.com.

For my eldest daughter

She inspires me each day to keep growing and reaching

for the stars.

Chapter 1

Anna Bolles took a sip of water to steady her nerves for the looming confrontation. Placing the glass bottle down on her desk, she continued to work on her end-of-day trades in an effort to leave her client files spot on. If she didn't seek out her boss soon, the opportunity for her to give notice at the investment firm of Blackly Simonson before the weekend would vanish. The five o'clock hour approached, and soon there would be a steadfast race for the pubs that surrounded the financial district in London.

A shiver ran down her spine, yet she made herself stand up. She needed to go through the proper protocol of declaring her resignation. I quit. I resign. I don't want to work here any longer. She carefully tucked her silk blouse into the waistband of her skirt and forced herself to walk over to Seth Aronson's office.

She deserved the opportunity to do something meaningful, something creative. She couldn't keep pushing aside her dreams and ambitions to satisfy others. She needed to let go of the expectations forced on her and decide what she wanted for her future.

Seth would remind her that working for Blackly Simonson was highly coveted and competitive, surviving the stressful environment was seen as a badge of honor, and those who thrived in it were well compensated. However, that line of thinking no longer mattered to her.

It wasn't as if she'd left herself any options. She had sold her expensive flat and was moving this weekend to a cheap, downtrodden neighborhood. And she had told her new employer that she would start Monday. Blackly Simonson would survive without her. She had completed all her back work and left copious notes on all of her clients' files.

Anna walked through the commercial accounts area, politely avoiding several of her colleagues who tried to engage her in conversation about plans for the evening.

She needed to do this, even if it meant risking her future. Smoothing down her gray skirt, she took in a restorative breath and handed her manager's assistant a sealed white envelope containing a letter that would officially sever her ties with Blackly Simonson.

Anna spoke briefly with the assistant and waited for her manager to finish his phone call before popping her head into his office. The walls were made of glass and her co-workers would be curious about her meeting with the Division Head.

Seth disconnected his call and stood. "Anna, this is a surprise. Is everything okay?"

She moved her long hair behind her shoulder. "I need to speak with you, if you have a moment."

"Wow. That sounds ominous." Seth gestured to a leather chair in front of his modern teak desk and sat down.

Dismissing the fluttering feeling in her chest, she slipped into the chair and forced herself to recite her practiced words. "I've decided to leave Blackly Simonson. Your assistant has my official letter of resignation."

Seth gave her an incredulous stare. Holding his hands up, he said, "I don't understand. You're brilliant at your job. The entire team has come to rely on you."

Anna touched her amethyst pendant necklace and tried to remain unemotional. She wanted this change and wouldn't allow Seth to use guilt or misplaced loyalty to entice her to stay. "I've been offered a position in a start-up. It's an events management company that has several prestigious clients. It's something totally different." She needed a different life. Blackly Simonson was slowly sucking the life out of her.

"You're choosing to leave for an events company?" The tone of his voice was agitated and sharp. He shook his head before continuing. "You have an advanced degree in mathematics from Oxford and can do the daily analysis and negotiation of trades in your sleep. And the fact that you are a Bolles has given you celebrity status at this firm."

She didn't expect him to welcome her decision. "There is no challenge for me. I may be good with numbers, but I'd rather use my creativity and have more freedom."

He leaned back in his chair. "I can give you more freedom."

She shook her head. "It's not the same. This place is about making money. I want something more meaningful." Her reasons sounded naïve or touchy-feely but she forced herself to hold his stare. She valued emotional connection more than dealing with statistics and market probability. She needed to take the steps to align her job with her values. The small events firm may be a misstep, but it was hers to make.

"Don't you feel any loyalty to the Bolles name? It has opened doors for you and sets you apart in this game."

Anna moistened her lips. "We're coming at this from different perspectives. And no, I don't feel any particular loyalty to my father's legacy."

Seth repeatedly tapped his hand on his desk. "As soon as the problems are solved at the start-up, then you'll be bored, Anna. You have the innate ability to understand complex financial calculations and the instinct to play the market and win."

He had a point. She had succeeded in the male-driven financial arena by having the best earnings ratio and being willing to take risks. But, instead of it bringing her joy, it brought her a sense of indifference. She didn't care about making more money.

She rose to her feet and was careful not to show weakness. He had been a supportive boss, stepping in and insisting the ego-driven young males treated her with respect. Many of the divisions didn't have the same leadership. "I'm sorry, Seth. I appreciate everything that you've done for me."

Seth bolted out of his seat. "You're making a mistake. Being a Bolles, the financial world is in your blood. By leaving, you are closing the door on a well-paid and respected career path. It doesn't make sense."

She may be a Bolles now, but when she was a child, she was nothing more than a shameful secret. "I know it must be difficult for you to understand. This place is everything to you, but not to me. Not any longer."

He flexed his shoulders. "Is this happening because the firm hired Sebastian Fox? I tried to prevent it."

Anna shook her head. She wasn't leaving because she was afraid of Sebastian. She had moved past the blackmailing incident, but it did show her that the firm valued performance over integrity. She had been going through the motions of building a successful career, but the firm employing a man capable of truly horrific deeds only served to make her take action. She would no longer overlook integrity issues in the pursuit of wealth. The sad truth was that her father lacked integrity, even though he had been enormously successful. She didn't want that type of life.

Seth lifted his phone and spoke in a resigned tone to security. Replacing the handset, he said, "Good luck, Anna. The door will always be open if you decide to return."

Seth had no control over the overarching polices of the Blackly Simonson. Every employee understood that the firm insisted that security escort anyone who gave notice out of the building. The act of leaving was viewed as disloyal and the company wanted to protect their client base.

Anna opened the glass door and a security officer met her in the hallway. Walking back to her cubicle, she picked up a small box from under her desk containing her personal belongings.

A hushed tone came over the cavernous space, and the man who sat next to her, Geoffrey Banks, said, "You gave notice?"

She nodded and took in the surprised and

perplexed looks from her colleagues. She needed a few minutes to process her conversation with Seth before she would be able to answer questions. While the business was competitive, they worked closely together. Since graduating university, all of her social interactions were focused on work.

One of her teammates called out, "Meet us at Martin's tonight."

She nodded. They wouldn't understand her decision, but would wish her well. She wasn't particularly keen to go to Martin's pub. She didn't want to bump into the owner, Alistair Martin. They had shared an awkward encounter years before and she had no desire to bump into him randomly. But, what were the chances of Alistair showing up at one of his pubs on the night she stopped in for a celebratory drink?

The security officer asked for her badge and ID and then searched her box of personal items. She wasn't taking anything from Blackly Simonson; in fact, she was leaving the financial world behind. She walked with the young security officer to the elevator.

Riding down to the lobby in a tense silence, a thousand thoughts flowed through her mind. By resigning, she was closing certain doors. She understood the financial world and it probably was in her genetics.

But she needed a change. She was tired of entertaining clients who drank too much and lived to party. She had worked extraordinarily hard for the company over the past three years, but with each passing day, she became more restless.

She nodded to the security officer and walked out

the front revolving door. Her life would change. Hopefully, for the better. She headed down the busy London sidewalk. It was closing time in the markets and the brokers and dealmakers were getting off work.

She noticed quite a few people gave her side-glances. Carrying the cardboard box in the busy rush hour crowd announced to absolute strangers that she either had been fired or had given notice.

A rush of adrenaline flowed through her body. She had actually told Seth. A smile took over her face.

Anna made her way over to a trash receptacle and, looking into the box, removed an antique letter opener, a pair of sunglasses, a silk scarf, and a few favorite pens and tucked them into her handbag. She tossed the remaining items, mostly lip balms and healthy snacks, into the trash and then took apart the box and placed it in a recycle bin. She had narrowly escaped a life where she was destined to prove something to others and finally considered her own ambitions.

Within a few short blocks, she walked into her building. Taking the elevator to the twelfth floor, she opened the door to her luxurious flat. The furnishings were mostly eclectic pieces, with an occasional traditional piece mixed in. She had decorated it herself and it was her first real venture into adulthood.

There were open boxes everywhere. The movers were coming Sunday to put most of her furniture in storage. She had found a cheap studio apartment in an old area of London. She would need to conserve every pound if she was going to be self-sufficient and be able to live on the small salary from the start-up for a year or more. Her savings would provide a safety net but she would no longer be able to count on large bonuses or automatic contributions to her retirement account.

She walked into the bedroom and stripped off her work clothes. She opted for a pair of low cut jeans and a button-down white cotton shirt. She pulled on black boots and left her long hair loose.

She glanced at her phone. Her co-workers were probably already waiting for her at the pub. Her mind wandered to an image of Alistair Martin. He was the definition of a wealthy entrepreneur who worked endlessly to build his empire. She'd caught a glimpse of him on Boxing Day, but sidestepped any possible conversation by hanging out with her young nieces and then disappearing before dinner. Her sister, Olivia, invited him to everything. It was nearly impossible to avoid him or avoid hearing about his antics and successes. Hopefully, tonight he was somewhere far away and not at his most popular pub.

Her body tightened. Afterwards, she would drop by her mother's house to share the news before someone else told her. It'd be an unwelcome and difficult conversation. She pushed away her worry. Elizabeth Harris was never truly happy about anything. Her daughter leaving Blackly Simonson would only add to her list of complaints.

She picked up her phone and called Frances Casey, her new partner and business associate, and relayed the good news. She was now free to throw herself into Gala & More. The two of them spoke briefly about upcoming events and then agreed to meet on Monday.

***

Walking into the pub a short while later, Anna saw that her former colleagues were already having a pint and good naturedly ranking on each other. Scanning the bar area, she didn't see Alistair and made an effort to relax her tight muscles.

One of her male colleagues, a man who could have stepped off the pages of GQ, said, "Anna, I can't believe you told Seth you're out."

Several of the people who gathered from her division nodded and looked at her.

Her cube mate, Geoffrey Banks, handed her a pint of Guinness and she took a swallow.

"It'll be a huge change." She smiled at Geoffrey. "I'll miss working with everyone."

"I didn't know you were actively looking for another job." He placed his bottle on the high table.

Geoffrey made the job look easy. He arrived at the office before anyone else and carefully planned out his workday. His questioning gaze made her realize that he felt slighted.

Anna looked at him. "I should have probably let on that I was considering a change. But I'm not staying in the industry. I took a position with a small events planning start-up called Gala & More."

Eric, a tall redhead that had been at the firm for a dozen years, said, "Bugger, Anna."

Everyone began asking her questions at once. Holding up her hand, she said, "It's a huge shift. I don't have a ton of experience with event planning, but I need something different. Something more creative and social."

Geoffrey touched his bottle to hers. "I wish you

the best of luck."

Watching the curious looks that everyone gave her, she could tell that they were uncertain about her career choice, but too polite to call her on it.

Anna took another sip of her Guinness. "I'll need it." She thought about Gala & More and her connection to Frances Casey. They had struck up an unlikely friendship more than a year ago when Frances reached out to her and asked for help. Hopefully, she could make a difference at the small company and help them grow the business.

The conversation shifted to the game on the large screen. When the keeper saved an impossible shot, a roar went up through the crowd gathered at the bar. Her co-workers were somewhat predictable. They adored sports and approached everything with a competitive angle, always wanting to know who had the advantage. It was both endearing and perplexing.

Will, a young professional who lived and breathed Blackly Simonson, said, "It's surprising. You had the top ranking in our division."

"I plan on seeking out other challenges for a while." Most of them would never understand her desire to move to an industry that wasn't about ranking or numbers.

Another goal was blocked and Geoffrey slapped Eric on the back and said, "Your team is going down, mate."

***

Alistair Martin walked into the pub and his eyes were drawn to a blond girl drinking a Guinness. Dressed in tight-fitting jeans and slim leather boots, her charming laugh and fit body set off a rapid-fire response within him. It was absurd; he had come in this evening to check on his new manager, not get caught up lusting after a patron.

He turned his attention back to his flagship microbrewery. The after-work crowd filled every available bar stool and spilled out to the tables and lounge area. He enjoyed the success of this place. It was his most lucrative pub.

Observing the wait staff, he could tell they were trying to warn each other. His expectations were tough but fair-minded. He had a reputation for an over-the-top work ethic and attention to the most minuscule detail. When he started out, that reputation was accurate, but these days he had scaled back slightly and allowed his management staff to make decisions and operate each establishment with autonomy.

His gaze returned to the group of investment bankers out for an after-work drink. The woman who captured his interest seemed to be at the center of the conversation and laughter. She had a familiar look but he could only see her profile. They were obviously celebrating something.

Why was he enthralled by this particular beauty in sexy jeans? Alistair stayed motionless as she turned and placed her empty bottle on the table and waved to the group. She walked straight towards him and he instantly recognized her. Anna Bolles. His best friend and her brother-in-law, Fionn Lynch, had declared her off-limits years ago. But, Alistair couldn't stop his traitorous body from wanting to seek her out.

She had a purely feminine appeal, with the sway of her hips and the graceful movement of long blond hair. Her face had only a trace of makeup, but she had a polished, elegant look about her. Their eyes met and she hesitated for a split second before continuing towards him.

She nodded in acknowledgment. "Mr. Martin, it's lovely to see you."

Her politeness grated on his nerves. Lovely was not the word he would use to describe their past encounters. Hot, sexy, and unresolved is how he would describe it. His body reacted to her nearness with a sensation of warmth spreading throughout all his veins.

"The pleasure is all mine." He looked into the crowd, trying to cool his reaction.

"I should go." She was inching away from him and the manager of the brewery in the distance tried to catch his attention.

He reached out and grasped her arm. "Can you stay for a drink?" Looking into her blue eyes, the breath in his chest stilled.

It was a stupid move. He should let her walk away. Anna Bolles had a hold over him. He had fantasized about her over the years more than he cared to admit. Her charming and seductive kisses had disturbed his dreams and made him yearn for more.

***

Anna moistened her lips. The last thing she needed tonight was to revisit her immature seduction of the great Alistair Martin. It was seven years ago, and when he'd realized she was Olivia's sister, he had completely and utterly rejected her.

She tucked a stray piece of hair behind her ear. "I'm not sure that would be wise."

Unfortunately, her teenage obsession with him

had never ended. These days, she was careful to keep away from him, which wasn't particularly difficult since he was work obsessed and avoided children's celebrations.

Alistair tightened his grip, halting her exit. A fluttering feeling took hold in her belly. Her heart raced and she could feel a nervous tension building in her stomach.

He moved closer to her. "We haven't properly talked in years."

Anna placed her hand on his arm and slipped out of his hold. "I can't imagine we have anything to say to one another."

The media covered him obsessively. Unfortunately, she would scan the internet for photographs of him when she had a spare moment and had closely followed all of his business ventures. Arrogance surrounded him. Alistair Martin dressed in expensive suits that clothed an extremely fit body. She had seen a tabloid image of him taken on the beach nearly a year ago and had studied his muscular yet slim build.

Fionn and her brother, William, talked about their adventures with Alistair playing in charity football matches and Iron Man competitions. When Alistair wasn't pursing physical challenges, he oversaw an extremely prosperous distillery empire and closely managed acres and acres of a third-generation winery in Southern England. He had always been a bit of a mystery to her. He held an advanced mathematics degree, but instead of seeking his fortune in the financial world, he chose agriculture and vice.

"I excel at small talk," he said.

She didn't. He would probably bring up her awkward attempt at seduction after drinking too much at Olivia's wedding. The hot encounter where he'd practically stripped her naked until he realized who she was. Somehow being Fionn's sister-in-law put her off-limits. He had asked her age and cursed when she had told him she was seventeen. After that, he barely looked at her. Instead, she ceased to exist in his world. Yet she craved the smallest glimpse of him.

Anna pushed her hair behind her shoulder. "I planned to see my mother this evening." She needed to escape his presence.

Alistair ran a hand through his short hair. "I'm hosting a charity gala at my house outside of London in a fortnight. Fionn and Olivia have promised to put in an appearance. Come with them."

He took a business card out of his pocket and handed it to her. She nodded and tucked it into her handbag. She wouldn't go. Her life was in turmoil, and she didn't need additional drama. Alistair had met her father, Oliver Bolles, several times before his tragic death in a motorcycle accident. There was bad blood between the families. It was too much of the past. She was trying to create a new life for herself.

Anna shrugged and, stepping away, said, "I'll try, but I'm rather busy with work at the moment."

He held her gaze a fraction too long, then said, "Possibly another time then," and smiled widely before saying, "Until our paths cross again."

"Until then. Cheerio." Anna moved away from him and headed towards the door.

Nothing good would come of her obsession with him. She forced herself to leave the brewery and walk the several blocks to her mother's brownstone. Attempting to banish the image of the strikingly handsome Alistair Martin from her mind, she thought about her mother's coming reaction to her change of careers.

Her new job would take every scrap of energy and focus. The start-up firm that hired her was short-handed and they were frantically trying to put together a launch party for a new magazine.

Anna thought about Frances Casey, who owned Gala & More and was about to go out on maternity leave. Olivia had pushed her to take the interview, telling her that the numerous events that she helped out with at the fashion house would be enough experience to throw herself into the start-up. But there was a huge difference between helping out in her spare time and being responsible for an entire event.

Ringing the doorbell at her mother's mansion, Anna took a deep breath and hoped her mother wouldn't make too big of a scene. She wasn't looking forward to the conversation, but she had learned that it was better to face issues head-on than trying to slowly finesse the outcome. Her father's deceptive behavior had scarred her. She had a steadfast need to tell the truth and she wouldn't allow herself to soften the message. Unfortunately, her mother relied on appearances and half-truths to conduct her life, so it wasn't always easy to have a heart-to-heart with her.

Her mother's housekeeper, Gertie, opened the door and ushered her in.

Gertie removed her apron. "So nice to see you, Miss Anna. Your mother is in the library."

She smiled at the older woman. "Thank you. You

as well. I hope things are good?"

Gertie had been working for her mother since Anna was twelve years old. She much preferred to chat with Gertie, as she was always warm and inviting. But, in this case, she needed to tell her mother the news herself.

"Yes. It's been quiet. Almost too quiet."

Anna touched Gertie's hand. "My mother has a way of inviting in drama, so maybe you should enjoy this small reprieve."

Gertie smiled and gestured towards the sitting room and headed back to the kitchen.

Gathering her reserves, Anna took in a deep breath and attempted to clear her mind. An image of Alistair Martin popped into her head. She couldn't believe after years of avoiding him, she turned around and he was standing there. On the day that she decided to risk her future and drastically change her life.

She pushed open the door to the formal living room and saw her mother sitting on the sofa.

Her mother looked up from the newspaper. "Anna, darling. I'm surprised to see you on a Friday night."

Stepping fully into the room, she put her handbag down on a nearby table. "Yes, well… something has come up and I wanted to talk with you."

Elizabeth Harris called out loudly, "Gertie, would you be a dear and bring Anna some tea?"

Anna felt her phone vibrate and read a text from Olivia. Did you give notice? She decided to ignore it for now and dropped her phone into her handbag.

Moving further into the room, she sat opposite her mother on a Victorian-style sofa. This wasn't going to go over well.

Pushing down the anxiety building in her stomach, Anna said, "Mother, I've come to a rather surprising decision and I hope you'll be able to listen with an open mind."

Elizabeth put the paper down and frowned. "It can't be good news or you wouldn't find it necessary to forestall my objections."

She met the older woman's unflinching gaze. "I know you've been proud of my accomplishments at Oxford and happy that I've been working for Blackly Simonson."

Her mother eyed her speculatively but remained silent, sipping her tea.

Gertie appeared with a small tray for her, and Anna accepted a hot cup of tea, waiting for the housekeeper to leave them. It was better not to drag her into the coming scene.

"Thank you, Gertie."

Anna took a sip and then placed the teacup down. "I gave notice today at Blackly Simonson and was escorted out of the building."

Her mother choked on her tea. Gasping, she asked, "Why would you do such a thing?"

"I've accepted a position as an events coordinator for a small start-up." Anna held up her hand. "The woman who launched the company is pregnant and needs to bring in a partner. It's just getting off the ground, but has a few prestigious clients."

Her mother's face tightened. "I don't understand. Why would you want to plan weddings and such?"

Anna took another sip of her tea. "It's not a wedding planning business. It's focused on corporate ventures. They have a contract to coordinate a show at the National Gallery in a few months and a launch for a new perfume."

"You intend to become a glorified party planner instead of working in the financial world?" Her mother's voice rose to fill the large room.

"I don't expect you to understand."

Elizabeth Harris valued wealth and appearance. There is no way her mother would understand her need to seek a different life.

"You're just like your father, secretive and selfish. You only do things that benefit you instead of thinking about others." Her mother's voice was brittle and harsh sounding.

Anna stood up. If she stayed longer, it would turn into a contest of wills with her mother trying to beat her down. "No. I'm nothing like my father. I may have inherited his talent for numbers but that is where the similarities end." She shouldn't have to defend herself to her mother.

Her mother's hand tightened on her teacup, causing it to rattle. "You'll be broke within a few months and I won't give you a pence towards your mortgage payments."

Anna knew enough to have contingency plans in place. Her mother was not one for helping out or supporting a new idea. "I've already sold my flat so I have sufficient reserves. I understand that this venture comes with risk, but if it doesn't work out then I'll do something else."

Her mother put her hand on her forehead. "If you cared for me at all then you wouldn't make a mockery of my sacrifices by throwing it all away."

Anna had heard this line of guilt so many times that it washed over her without hitting its mark. She had done everything her mother had required of her, even when it went against her natural inclinations. She had frozen her father out of her life because Elizabeth had demanded it. She had wanted to accept him for who he was and have some type of connection to him. But her mother forbade it. Now it was too late. He had died when she was seventeen.

"I'll text you my new address and work information."

Her mother stood. "You shouldn't have sold your flat. It was in one of the best buildings in London."

If she held onto it, it would have kept her locked in a path that no longer had any meaning. "I wouldn't have been able to afford the mortgage on the small salary that I'll earn for a while."

"You're making a colossal mistake." Her mother's negativity slammed against her as if she stepped on the tines of a rake and the resulting force hit her square in the face.

She kept her voice neutral. "It's mine to make, mother."

"I hope you come to your senses." Her mother picked up her newspaper and turned to another page.

"Goodnight." Anna could feel the tension in every muscle of her body. Walking out the front door, she wished their relationship could be less adversarial.

She cared for her mother, but the bitter woman saw the world so differently. Elizabeth Harris cared about appearances. Her father deceiving them with his double life hadn't helped. Her mother had only become more rigid and unforgiving. Being an only child put enormous pressure on Anna to please her mother. She was a natural scholar, so it became a game to achieve academic excellence. By choosing a different life, she was setting clear boundaries and opening herself up to new experiences.

She wanted more from life than finding success in the financial markets. She hated to think about her father, but forced herself to consider why he failed at close relationships. Her father pretended he was averse to commitment, but he had a family in London and a wife and son in New York, and another daughter being raised by a guardian in Ireland. Was it any surprise that she had difficulty trusting others?

Anna pushed the negative thoughts from her mind. She would head over to see her sister and her nieces. Olivia understood her need to create something that was uniquely hers. And her young nieces were a joy to be around.

      ***

Ringing the doorbell at her sister's house, she waited only a minute before her little niece greeted her.

Stepping inside Olivia's townhouse, the memory of kissing Alistair in the back garden popped into her head. It had been an uncharacteristic moment of madness. She always did the right thing and didn't seek out male attention. But, that evening she had acted like a complete and utter fool.

"Auntie Anna, have you come for my bath time?" The small blond girl reminded her of herself as a child.

She scooped the five-year-old into her arms amid a flurry of giggles, saying, "I'd love to give you your bath."

Olivia appeared with her two-year-old in her arms. "Fionn has a late flight so we can chat once these two lovelies are in bed."

After a drawn-out bedtime routine, she and Olivia stretched out on the sofa, each with a glass of chardonnay.

"Beatrix and Ady are delightful, Liv."

"They're missing Fionn, but somehow we survived the week."

Her sister looked happy. Even juggling a successful fashion business, motherhood, and an endless romantic fascination with Fionn, her husband, she looked calm and rested.

Anna bit her lip and nodded. "I told Seth Aronson today."

Her sister raised her eyebrows. "You resigned?"

Taking a sip of wine, Anna said, "Yes. I sold my flat and decided to accept the job. It's going to be feast or famine for a period of time, but I'll make it work."

"If you need any help, let Fionn and I know and we can advance you enough money."

Anna looked down at her glass. Olivia cared about her and had enormous resources but she wanted to succeed on your own. She didn't want her family's help.

Olivia touched her glass to hers. "Congratulations. You'll be amazing at events planning."

She let out a huge breath. "I even stopped in and told my mother. I was just working up to it when I got your text."

Olivia grimaced. "That couldn't have been pleasant."

Anna took another sip of her wine. "She didn't take it particularly well."

Olivia placed her glass on the ornate table. "You have to silence the naysayers and follow your instincts."

The two sat in silence for a few minutes, each lost in thought.

Anna glanced at her phone. "I ran into Alistair Martin at his brewery this evening. I didn't think he spent much time there. But, he invited me to a gala at his house and mentioned you and Fionn are going."

Olivia nodded. "He does an annual black tie fundraiser for homeless and disadvantaged youth."

Anna met her sister's gaze. "He's quite a saint."

Olivia shook her head. "It'd be a good networking opportunity for you. You'll need to begin thinking about bringing in future clients. Landing his account would be tremendous for your new company."

She leaned forward and placed her glass on the cocktail table. "I'm sure Alistair has in-house staff to coordinate his events. He wouldn't take a risk on a start-up venture."

"The man is all about risk." Olivia winked at her.

"I doubt he takes risks with his business." If she wasn't careful, her sister would slip into matchmaking mode, when what Anna needed was to oust her teenage fantasy of Alistair Martin from her life and move forward.

For too many years, she'd carefully avoided him and his rejection. She needed to banish him from her dreams. After coming face-to-face with him tonight, it would be harder. The excitement from seeing him earlier in the evening eclipsed all other feelings. The excitement continued to heighten her awareness.

Olivia went into the kitchen and came back with a bowl of cherries. "As you know, Alistair is a good friend of Fionn's. I'm sure Fionn would be willing to approach him for you. In the wine industry, there must be tons of events."

The last thing she needed was to be thrown into Alistair's path. The man was unforgiving and intense. "Maybe in the future. I need to find my footing before seeking out such a well-known client."

Her sister looked at her speculatively. "You've always been a little odd around Alistair. It's almost as if you avoid him."

Anna shifted her position on the sofa. "We had an awkward encounter at your wedding and I prefer to keep a safe distance." She remembered the passionate kisses in the back garden, in her mind, she could see the fig tree where she had thrown herself at him.

Olivia's hand flew to her chest. "Was he rude to you?"

She shook her head. "No. Actually quite the opposite. I fancied him, and after sneaking a glass of champagne, I kissed him and he took me in his arms and kissed me back."

Olivia reached out and touched her arm. "I had no idea. What happened?"

"I don't think he knew who I was at that point. After a few exploratory kisses in the darkness, Fionn called my name and he stepped back, surprised."

"Oh." Olivia frowned.

"Yes. He couldn't get away fast enough."

Olivia looked at her softly. "You may be reading too much into it. It was years ago and a few stolen kisses. I doubt he thinks about it."

Anna shook her head. "Alistair lectured me about modesty and not encouraging advances that I wasn't ready to handle."

Olivia gave her a searching look and then placed her hand on hers. "I'm sorry, Anna. That does sound awkward. But, it was a long time ago. You were a teenager and Alistair must have been surprised by your age."

"I agree." She had tried to forget about Alistair Martin, but for some odd reason, he fascinated her. Deciding to change the subject, she asked Olivia, "Do you have any advice on the start-up?"

Olivia sat back and crossed her legs. "If you're serious about succeeding with this start-up, then you'll need to use your contacts to find work. There will be many titans of business at the gala. Go and network. I'll help you."

The conversation moved to the fashion business and they chatted for a long while about the upcoming season. Anna helped her sister brainstorm about possible venues for a boutique show until they heard Fionn unlock the door.

Anna stood up and hugged her sister. "I know you must be tired. I'll call you later in the week."

Fionn came in and greeted them both.

Olivia smiled. "Good luck this week. You should keep Alistair in mind, he could introduce you to some of his contacts."

Fionn removed his suit jacket and tie. "That's probably not a good idea, Liv."

Raising her eyebrows, Olivia said softly, "Men had a way of growing up."

Anna walked towards the front door. "Cheers. See you both soon."

Anna was sure he had no interest in seeing her get involved with his childhood friend. Fionn was an over-protective brother-in-law and would sometimes treat her as if she were a child. She loved that he cared, but she needed her freedom and the space to make her own decisions.

She walked to the metro and acknowledged to herself that finding out she had two grown siblings was the best thing that could have happened to her. She hadn't resented them for very long. Her life had been so lonely that she instead embraced them fully within a few months of meeting them. Olivia was kind and nurturing. She had taken Anna under her wing and had stayed involved through all of the difficulties of her life. Her brother, William, was sheer fun. He was the same age and was always encouraging her to let her hair down and add some pleasure to her life. Without them, she might have allowed herself to not fully live. But now, with the changes ahead, that wasn't an option for her. They inspired her to explore her talents and ambitions.

Contemplating the week ahead, Anna realized there was a ton to do. The movers were coming on Sunday and she needed to have everything packed up. She tried to banish thoughts of Alistair from her mind, but kept replaying the chance meeting in her head. She needed to stop obsessing about him. The move and her new job were going to be challenging enough and she needed to focus on her future.

Chapter 2

On Monday morning, Anna walked the four blocks to the Gala & More office from her new flat. Crossing the street, she purposely didn't make eye contact with police roping off a crime scene. The neighborhood was mixed commercial and residential, and unfortunately, wasn't considered up-and-coming.

Her cramped, walk-up second-floor flat needed her attention, but it would have to wait. Frances would be going out on maternity leave soon and she needed to throw herself into the new venture.

Feeling her mobile beep in her pocket, she took it out and read a text from Olivia about attending the fundraising gala at Alistair's house. She shouldn't have told her sister about Alistair. Olivia would relentlessly question it. Tucking the phone back into her handbag, she decided to answer her sister later.

Frances had given her a key so she could arrive early and begin to think about changes. They had agreed that the company would need to relocate in the future if they intended to garner any respect.

Anna stopped in front of the building and glanced up. It looked dilapidated. Taking the key from her handbag, she walked up four stone steps and struggled to get the old key into the lock. After several attempts, she managed to open the door. Looking around, she saw junk everywhere, along with piles of paper and rubbish.

Closing the door behind her, she stepped further into the office space. Her nose wrinkled at the offensive odor. She couldn't tell if the smell reminded her of mold or rot.

Turning the lights on, she saw water stains on the old, dirty carpet. She would need to call a plumber.

The office phone began to ring. The receptionist didn't start until ten o'clock, so Anna walked over and picked up the phone on the fourth ring. She jotted a message down from an irate client. It couldn't be a good sign. Going into the conference room, she unpacked her laptop and started picking up rubbish. How could the office be so bloody disorganized?

Anna didn't know where to begin. She started opening closets and cabinets, looking for a box of trash bags. She opened a large closet in the hall and items began falling out. A broom and ironing board blocked her path. Taking them out of the closet, she set them in the hall.

A young woman came in well after ten o'clock and explained that she had childcare issues and that the other employee, Elyse, had taken a few days off.

The woman said, "It looks better in here. I'm Katie, by the way."

"Hello, Katie. I'm Anna, but you probably guessed that." Anna continued removing rubbish. "Did you know that there's a leak?"

Katie looked at the ceiling. "I think it only leaks when the couple in the apartment upstairs gives their dog a bath."

Anna looked at the young receptionist. Water damage was hugely problematic. It could mean mold, or at the very least damaged equipment or items.

Going into the bathroom, she washed her hands. Looking down at her clothing, it looked as if she had cleaned a chimney. She should have worn old clothes instead of her stylish skirt and blouse. A layer of dust and grime coated her exposed skin.

Coming back into the main area, Anna said, "I may need to reach the owner and ask that the ceiling get repaired." She pointed to the wet stack of tablecloths. "How will these get cleaned?"

Katie was looking for something on her desk. "A linen service collects items on Wednesday. It'll be fine."

Anna let out a heavy sigh. "The office doesn't seem adequate enough to invite in prospective clients. How can Frances bring anyone here?"

Katie slipped her hands into her pockets. "She normally meets clients at coffee houses. This building is somewhat run-down and she brings her dog to work, so it's not a perfect environment for meetings."

Anna nodded. That explained the dog hair everywhere. She remembered meeting Frances at a coffee house around the corner. She should have asked to see the office. This place was the complete opposite of Blackly Simonson.

"Right. Well, I took a few messages this morning."

She handed Katie a few pieces of paper and tried to decide what she should tackle next.

"Is there a lunch area?"

Katie pointed to a corner of the office with an old

coffee pot and stacks of recycling. "The coffee pot probably needs to be cleaned. It hasn't been used recently."

"Is there a schedule for the week?" Anna had already made list of upcoming events and started filling in the required tasks.

Katie looked puzzled. "Usually Frances decides what to do when she gets here."

Anna began calculating the cost of a massive renovation along with hiring an experienced assistant. Katie was friendly and upbeat but worked part-time.

"Do you think Elyse is coming in next week? It's rather odd for her to be taking time off this week."

"Things are a bit up in the air. In fact, Elyse has mentioned interviewing elsewhere."

There was no way Anna could keep the company going if the only person who knew anything gave notice. "Can you get her on the phone for me?"

Katie gave her a dazed look. "I'm not sure that it's a good idea. Elyse needs time to manage the change."

Elyse was probably worried about someone new coming in and taking over. "I'm sure it'll be fine. If she is interviewing elsewhere, I need to know."

Anna moved her laptop over to a table by the window. There were two important meetings that week and, before she moved forward, she had to come up with a strategy. The financials needed work and it seemed as if there wasn't a clear process for how each event was being quoted. Accessing the billing software, she could tell that Frances was getting projects by bidding too low.

Katie called out, "Elyse is on line two."

Anna spoke with Elyse and asked her to come by for coffee that afternoon. The conversation was stilted, but she was careful to stay encouraging and positive. She would promise Elyse anything if she was willing to stay on a minimum of three months.

Next, she called Frances and spoke at length about the business. Frances let her know that she had an emergency doctor's appointment, but hopefully would be in the next day. They discussed the possibility of finding an investor to bring cash into the business.

Anna called each client and insisted on a budget review meeting. By the end of the day, she was discouraged by the lack of structure in the small company, and the books told a much different story than Frances had let on. Unless something drastically changed, they would be out of business within a month or two. This was not what she had in mind in terms of a new start. If she wasn't careful, she would be overseeing the demise of a company.

***

Anna met with Frances and Katie the next morning. They discussed the details for a fundraising event at a community library. She could tell that the creativity part of the business was thriving. They both had amazing ideas and concepts for putting together a memorable event.

Frances had short dark hair and a beautiful smile. She wore fitted clothing over her round belly and said, "The midwife warned me that I could go early."

Anna crossed her arms. "Without you or Elyse here, I don't know how I'll be able to do anything."

Frances swept her hand over the messy space.

"I've been completely knackered. But we have notes on everything and we can chat whenever you have questions."

"I've never seen a more disorganized office space," Anna said, glancing around the office. "Client files aren't put away, so I have to search through stack after stack."

Frances sat down slowly, supporting her huge belly. "A start-up is much different than a Financial Services firm. Sometimes, it's pure bedlam. You've got to somehow deal with that."

"You may need to consider closing down for now, and in the future, you can try again." Anna hated making the suggestion, but the business was not sound.

Frances steadily stroked her belly. "As I mentioned yesterday, we've been invited to a pitch session for an investment group that could potentially offer funding for the company. We need some stability. If you could get together a presentation, then Gala & More Event Planning could be properly funded. That would solve many of the issues."

"You'll have to relinquish control while you're on maternity leave," Anna said. "I can't become responsible for everything and not have decision-making powers."

Frances stood up slowly. "Anna, if you're successful in getting the funding and running the company in my absence for six months, then I'll give you a fifty percent stake."

Anna hesitated. Why would Frances give up fifty percent of the ownership? She must think that it was the only path forward.

After a brief hesitation, she held out her hand and Frances shook it.

She looked at Frances. "I'm a little worried." But the competitive part of her wanted to dig her heels in and help the company survive.

They spent the remaining part of the day and the next pulling together event information and discussing the pitch.

On Friday morning, Anna received a text that Frances was in labor. Anna had convinced Elyse to stay on, but the weekend had two events. She hoped when she went onsite that the planning was adequate and she wouldn't be overseeing a disaster. The most important thing on the agenda was the upcoming pitch session. Without funding, she didn't think the company would survive. She would hate to see Gala & More fail while Frances was home with a new baby.

***

Five days later, Anna arrived at the five-star hotel a few minutes early for the pitch session. She had gone over the financials a dozen times and hoped whoever she was pitching to would be interested in an events management company.

She followed the signs to a conference room on the second floor.

Mentally reviewing the list of requirements for the pitch session, she attempted to organize her thoughts. She had emailed the presentation and documents ahead of time, and was ready to give a short presentation on Gala & More. She had been told to expect eight to ten investors in the room for her pitch.

A well-dressed man asked for her business card

and then said, "You have a few minutes, Ms. Bolles, before you can go in. I have a list of the investors that are here today. Please remember the information is confidential and not to be shared." He handed her a list of names and when she scanned the list, her heart plummeted.

"Is everything okay?"

Nodding her head, she tried to take in a deep breath. Why would Alistair Martin be on the list? How could she be so unlucky that he would choose her pitch to evaluate? She was doomed. There was no way she could go on with the pitch. He would never take her seriously.

Anna had been at Gala & More less than two weeks. She had no real experience with event management. He would rake her over the coals.

Waiting in line to go in, she attempted to relax her shoulders and smile. She contemplated whispering an excuse to the assistant organizing the presenters and slipping out of the hotel. But, she needed to show confidence if she was to have any chance of securing the much-needed funding.

When the assistant nodded to her, Anna pretended a confidence she didn't feel. She visualized Frances holding her beautiful baby girl and reminded herself that much was riding on this ten-minute session.

She wore a fitted charcoal linen dress with sheer stockings and expensive heels. Her long hair was up in a twist. Her goal was to look professional, yet stylish. She had practiced her pitch several times and hoped the words would flow and the investors would be inclined to select Gala & More.

Anna opened the door and avoided eye contact with Alistair. She could see the seven men seated behind a massive wood table and chose a point just above their heads to focus on. The room had been set up with a smart board, laptop, and a pitcher of water and a glass.

The business plan she had created was printed and bound, set neatly in front of each potential investor.

There was a technician off to the side, ready to place a microphone on her. She stood patiently and collected her thoughts while he hooked up the connections and handed her a remote to control the presentation.

The splash screen had Gala & More on it and she pressed the button to advance the slide.

"Hello, gentleman. My name is Anna Bolles and I'm pitching for Gala & More today."

"Are you set on the name?" Alistair asked, making a notation on his notepad.

She hesitated for a brief moment. "Gala & More requires funding, but has already garnered some name recognition, so I don't know that it would be a wise move to change the name." She could feel her palms getting sweaty.

Alistair twirled a pen in his hand. "Why don't you give us your five-minute elevator pitch and then we'll ask questions?"

Why did she feel so on edge in his presence? He had the look of an Irish model combined with a keen intellect. She had gone to school and worked with countless men who could have been models and none of them caused this reaction.

If she wasn't careful, every thought would leave her mind and she would be a bumbling mess.

Smoothing a strand of hair away from her face, Anna said, "Before I start, I didn't know who I would be pitching to and, given the fact that we have met socially, Mr. Martin, I wonder if that is in any way a conflict of interest. At the very least, I feel it is important to acknowledge the connection."

She watched the other men glance at Alistair.

He met her gaze. "We were expecting Frances Casey. Given the fact that you're a Bolles, I bet everyone on the panel has had a connection to you or your father." He remained silent for a moment before continuing. "I don't think it's relevant. Don't make the mistake of thinking that it'll give you an advantage. We keep the membership of the network confidential so we don't attract scores of propositions. Now, if you are ready to proceed?"

***

How was he possibly going to remain neutral? Alistair had been fantasizing about her since their chance encounter at the brewery. He had no idea she had signed onto a start-up company.

There was a physical attraction between them that she had acted on years ago, but he hadn't been able to allow himself the pleasure of pursuing her. Fionn Lynch had warned him off. He had a protective streak towards his sister-in-law and no intention of allowing Alistair to seduce her.

But something told him that Fionn had no idea how resistant and tough Anna Bolles was. He had been watching her career, and she was known as a brilliant and talented broker. Why would she jump ship and want to own part of an events management company?

He listened to her give an overview of their clients and early successes. Her voice soothed his raw nerves. She was a huge distraction. He could barely take in her words; instead, he was drawn to the beautiful lines of her body and graceful gestures she made with her hands.

"Where is the founding partner, Frances Casey?" He interrupted her as he read her name from the slide.

"Ms. Casey is on maternity leave."

Alistair made a dismissive gesture with his hand. "You expect us to fund a company that you joined a week ago?"

Anna folded her hands together and faced the panel. "I've been in conversations with Ms. Casey for some time and planned to come on board when she stepped back to take leave."

He leaned back in his chair. "Didn't you work insane hours at Blackly Simonson until recently?" Why was he allowing her to get under his skin?

She nodded. "Yes. But, I managed to find time to help with various parties and events."

She held up her hand to forestall his next objection. "Mr. Martin, the skill set I bring to Gala & More is leadership and financial literacy, not event management."

He sat forward. "Are you implying Ms. Casey is financially illiterate?" He suppressed a smile. Unfortunately, she was even more beautiful when she was on the defensive and actively backpedaling.

"No. I'm not implying that. However, she is a creative genius and it's not possible to do everything extremely well. Within our partnership, I'm more practical or budget-oriented, while she's more of a visionary."

Anna advanced the slide and he sat back and allowed her to finish.

***

Her hands were shaking when she ended the presentation. It was impossible to know what the investors were thinking. It reminded Anna of a poker game, with everyone being careful to not show their cards just yet. Most of the questions were about the financials and she easily answered them.

Alistair took the lead. "So you're seeking a five-year investment, 250,000 pounds sterling at eight percent?"

One of the men who had been silent said, "Ms. Bolles, we invest in start-ups who give back to the community. Beyond hiring different catering and staging firms, you have not been able to sufficiently justify how your company would benefit the local community."

Anna moved away from the podium. "I wanted to concentrate on the business concept and numbers first, because to give back a company needs to be successful. Ms. Casey and I intend to donate our time and expertize to five community organizations each year that serve underprivileged members of society. For example, there are wonderful soup kitchens that go unnoticed. We want to help them gain recognition and funding by putting together fundraising or publicity events for them."

The man held up his hands and said, "That's all the questions I have."

It was possible that they liked the concept but

would choose not to invest. She wished there were a few women on the panel. Most of these men were probably tired of dressing up and attending galas. They probably didn't see the importance of an events company.

Anna stepped forward. "Celebrations are important in life. It's how progress is measured, it encourages people to meet milestones, and can give some inspiration to keep working. I know all of you are successful business owners. You should ask yourself—where would your business be if you didn't celebrate important milestones or achievements? Gala & More seeks to help businesses acknowledge hard work and encourages employees to keep moving forward."

Alistair met her gaze. "Well said. But there is tough competition in London for an events planning business. For some reason, the city appeals to a wide range of party enthusiasts."

She straightened her spine. "Based on the type of clients we have secured, Gala & More does appeal to a range of clients, from museums to cosmetics companies. We need the proper funding to create a lasting entity."

Alistair tapped his pen on the notepad. "I have an unusual proposition for you. I'm not ready to invest, but I am strangely reluctant to say no."

Anna took a deep breath. What could he possibly mean? Her pitch fit the parameters for investment and Gala & More had several high-profile clients.

He continued, "You are rather new to the venture and Ms. Casey is on leave. I'd like to see you in action at an event you design and coordinate. Call my office and set up an appointment for next week. We can discuss the terms then."

She wanted to decline his offer, but Gala & More needed a lifeline. What possible hoops would he want her to jump through? There was so much to do and not enough time as it was. No one else came forward, so she was stuck with a possible offer with contingencies.

Anna nodded. "Thank you, everyone, for your time and consideration."

She left the podium and the technician came forward to remove her microphone. Stepping out of the door, she smiled at the two young men ready to go in.

Pulling out her phone, she waited a moment before texting Frances. The meeting hadn't ended with an offer for financing but it also hadn't been an outright rejection. She glanced at the time. Alistair could still decide not to invest. The last thing she needed was to meet with him alone. She had a hard enough time putting him out of her mind.

Texting Frances the outcome, Anna grabbed a taxi back to the office to deal with the hundreds of tasks waiting for her.

***

A week later, Anna walked into Martin Enterprises and marveled at the difference between a business of wineries and breweries as opposed to the financial world. The atmosphere was less pressurized and more about interaction. There were beautiful photographs of the vineyards in the main lobby and a floor-to-ceiling display of wine bottles behind glass. There were also glass cases displaying the tools of the trade.

The receptionist guided her to the fourth floor of the historic building. Stepping off the elevator, she was greeted by another receptionist and invited to wait in a luxurious seating area. Picking up a magazine about the wine trade, she flipped through the pages and waited for the great Alistair Martin to find time to see her.

She should feel grateful that he was giving her an opportunity to further discuss the investment, but instead she was defensive and irritated.

He came out into the lobby.

"Ms. Bolles?"

She stood and shook his hand. "I appreciate you seeing me."

Instead of dressing up for the meeting, she wore a white button-down shirt with grey dress pants. She had put her hair in a ponytail and applied only a minimal amount of makeup. She didn't want to give him the impression that she was trying too hard.

Alistair led her to a spacious office with plate glass windows overlooking the River Thames. His corporate offices were located thirty minutes from London, giving him tremendous views and more square footage. But, his office had been a challenge to get to without a car. She opted to use a taxi, but the driver wasn't thrilled and wouldn't commit to coming back for her.

"Would you care for a glass of wine?" He pulled out a bottle of sauvignon and effortlessly opened the cork.

Why did he make her so nervous? "Please."

"So polite. Some people are irritated to leave London during the work day."

"Why would I be irritated?" She breathed in his clean scent when he handed her the wine. She should distance herself and not be so enamored with him. It'd not help her case at all if she hung on his every word like a schoolgirl with an obsessive crush.

He stood next to her and steadily held her gaze. "I doubt you are told no often."

Her eyes widened. Was he referencing their seductive encounter years ago? She couldn't imagine what else he would be referring to. "I've been told no repeatedly in my life."

He raised his eyebrows in response. "As Oliver's daughter, you must have grown up living a life of extreme privilege. Private boarding schools, equestrian competitions, staff to accommodate your every wish."

She crossed her arms. He obviously knew nothing about her upbringing, but she refused to share intimate details about her childhood. She didn't have any affinity with horses. In fact, they scared her. "You're against wealth? Isn't that slightly contradictory? Seeing how you're an immensely successful businessman." Why did he have to stand so close to her? Her nerves were on edge as it was.

He lowered his voice slightly. "When it prevents someone from seeing reality." He paused and her awareness of him became overwhelming. "A start-up is very different than a prestigious position in the financial world."

Anna moved away from him and sat down in a chair near his desk and crossed her legs. "I understand that a different skill set is needed for a start-up. I was drawn to either starting my own venture or joining a start-up because I wanted greater freedom and autonomy. But it also happens that my financial background brings a necessary skill set to the table."

Alistair stretched out in the chair next to her. "I check the background of every company that I fund. Gala & More is a long shot. But instead of simply turning down the deal, I'm going to give you the opportunity to prove yourself."

Anna touched her neck. "I'm not sure what you mean." Why did he want to challenge her?

He looked out over the river before glancing back at her. "I'm willing to give Gala & More a contract to put together a harvesting celebration."

She narrowed her eyes. "Why would you hire us if you are uncertain of investing?"

He smiled and she had the impression he was leading her down this path to see if she would fail.

Alistair formed a steeple with his hands. "Martin Enterprises has a new wine that we intend to introduce at this event. If the event is successful, then I'll fund Gala & More. If I'm not satisfied with the ideas, orchestration, or anything else, then we'll part ways. No harm done."

Why would he waste his time if he wasn't interested in investing? Was it possible that he had an old score to settle with the Bolles family? He wouldn't be the first person who wanted to seek some sort of retaliation against her father.

She pushed aside her reservations and considered his challenge. Instead of overthinking it, she should just accept it at face value. It'd be good for the company either way. Knowing that he was judging them would add another layer of stress, but if they were successful, it'd be worth the added work because they would be properly funded.

He watched her with an alert gaze. "This weekend is the fundraiser that I'm hosting. I mentioned it a few weeks ago. I expect you to attend. You'll need to immerse yourself in Martin Enterprises."

She touched the stem of her wine glass, feeling self-conscious with his eyes on her. "I'll need to check my schedule. Can you give me more details about the event you expect Gala & More to put together?"

He smiled at her. "Maybe I should find out more about Gala & More first."

"What do you want to know?" she asked, glancing at the window, the desk, anywhere but at him. "You've looked over the financials, background of the partners, and during the presentation I discussed recent events we coordinated."

Alistair exuded an air of unruffled confidence and focus. "I'd like to see your offices and the systems you use to organize events."

She made an effort to unclasp her hands. "You must know from the address that the office is in a shabby, low-rent neighborhood. It's not meant as a place to bring clients. With proper funding, we plan to rent a more suitable space." There was no way she would give him a tour of the office; it was hideous and would not reflect well on the company.

He stood up. "I've no issue with starting from nothing. In fact, it can be a good practice to keep your overhead low. I insist on seeing the company office and meeting the employees. We could head there now."

She shook her head. "It's late in the day, so the

staff has gone home."

He glanced at his watch. "It's not even five o'clock."

Anna got to her feet and turned towards him. "We're an events company. The staff works evenings and weekends, so there is flexibility during the work week."

He picked up his keys. "I'll drive you back to London and you can at least show me the office space."

She crossed her arms. "I ... can't do that."

"Why not?"

Either she'd refuse and the funding would fall apart or she'd placate him and he would question their professionalism and her ability to run a company.

"I need a week before I show you the office space. Quite honestly, I've been focusing on other aspects of Gala & More and haven't had the opportunity to deal with the hoarding situation at the office." Hopefully, her honesty wasn't going to be a deal breaker.

***

He gave her credit for her truthfulness. His assistant had visited the location and the report was not positive. He didn't want her to fail—she was obviously hardworking and dedicated—but it would take more than those traits to resurrect Gala & More. She would need top-notch public relations skills, perseverance, and creative ideas.

Alistair wasn't in the habit of being swayed by a personal agenda, but he was drawn to Anna. His instincts told him that she'd surprise everyone. There was an edge to her. Even though she was raised with privilege, she was a fighter. If she weren't off limits, he would be pursuing her for himself.

"Shall we say next Tuesday in the morning? There is a wine event that evening that I would like you to attend with me."

Anna looked at her phone and checked the date.

Without looking up, she asked, "How many events do you expect me to attend?"

Why was she reluctant to spend time with him? He kept the impatience out of his voice. "As many as it takes to give you a sense of the industry, the expectations, and ideas for a memorable celebration."

She met his gaze and he could feel his blood heat. They had an unbelievable chemistry between them. He banished an image of her naked and willing in his bed. Their association couldn't be about desire and sex. He needed to keep a level head and curtail his curiosity. Her connection to Fionn should be enough to keep his hands off of her. He owned Fionn more than he could ever repay.

She scrolled through her calendar. "Do you have the date and budget set?"

Anna Bolles may be off-limits, but he was going to enjoy watching her jump through hoops for him. "Mid-October, and the budget will depend on the concept, the venue, and catering."

She placed her phone in her bag. "It's a long time to wait for a decision about investing."

"You're free to explore other options." He wouldn't make this too easy for her. If he was going to invest, he wanted to know that she could build a company and overcome obstacles.

Her eyes flashed a blue fire and she barely

contained her frustration. "I'd rather not spend my time looking for funding."

"I agree with you. It can be a waste of time getting caught up in seeking investment endlessly." He should cut her some slack. Her sister was married to his best friend, but in business, it was best to leave personal associations out of it. He invested to see a substantial return, not out of sentiment.

He checked the time. "I'm going into London this evening and can give you a lift home."

She met his gaze. "I can call a taxi."

A powerful lust shot through him. Watching her lick her lips, he wanted to taste the fragrant blend of wine on her mouth. He turned away from her and tried to dispel his desire. What was it about her that drew him in? It wasn't her connection to Oliver Bolles. He had disliked her father the few times he had met him. There was bad blood between the Bolles family and his grandparents. They rarely talked about it, but he assumed it had something to do with his father and his insatiable need to gamble away everything.

Turning back towards her, Alistair asked, "What did you think of the wine?"

She placed her glass on the table. "I thought it was delicious."

It brought him enormous satisfaction when someone enjoyed the wine from his vineyard. He had worked endless hours over the last decade to bring his grandparent's vineyard back into prominence. His father had destroyed its reputation and nearly forced it into bankruptcy.

"Why don't I drive you back? I'll give us more time to talk."

Anna nodded and picked up her bag.

He guided her out of the back entrance of the building to his Land Rover.

***

Sliding into the luxurious leather seat, Anna attempted to relax. Olivia would find her predicament funny. The other night her sister had mentioned that Alistair could introduce her to his contacts. Fionn had just walked in and wasn't thrilled with the exchange. He didn't want her to get involved with Alistair, and his wife playfully suggested that men had a way of growing up.

Fionn had mentioned years ago that Alistair had been raised by a single mother in Ireland, and it was not until his father died that his grandparents reached out to him. She guessed his parents never married and his mother was important in his life. She had also heard that Alistair ran wild on the streets of Dublin with Fionn but excelled at academics. He had been given a scholarship to attend an elite boarding school in London.

Alistair skillfully navigated the rush hour traffic flowing into London. He didn't become impatient when made to wait. She vaguely remembered driving with her father in London when she was a child, and he would become enraged if another driver cut in front of him.

He turned off the radio. "So, you intend to use the next few days to deal with the hoarding tendencies of your colleagues?"

Beyond hiring a refuse company to remove everything, she hadn't formulated a plan yet. "It has to be dealt with. We wouldn't want to hire a lorry to move the junk to a new location in the future."

Alistair laughed. It was a low, throaty laugh that calmed her nerves slightly.

She checked her calendar. "I have an afternoon event on Saturday, so I'll be a little late for your gala."

He glanced at her. "Have you talked to Olivia and Fionn recently?"

She thought about her sister. She was immensely grateful to have such a loving sister and nieces. Her life would be so different without them. "Yes. I talk with her most days. Olivia is incredibly generous, which has saved me on numerous occasions."

"I haven't seen Fionn and Olivia in months. How is their wedded bliss going?" he asked in a distracted tone.

She looked out the window. "Pretty blissful. They are enjoying their girls and of course are busy with their empires."

"Why didn't you approach Fionn to fund your new venture?" His direct question surprised her. Did Alistair feel competitive towards Fionn?

"I want to do it on my own. I don't agree with mixing money and family members. It could get complicated if things didn't go according to plan or if there is a difference of opinion."

Alistair downshifted and moved lanes. He gave her a slow smile. "It's odd how our paths have crossed again in a business setting instead of through our more personal connection."

Anna nodded. "I agree."

It was odd and a complication she could have done without. Being near him made her forget all of the carefully developed rules she had about men. It made her wish for things that were impossible. Given the chance, she would throw herself at him again. But, she was older and wiser this time and knew enough to hold back. Life wasn't full of happy endings. Her father and mother had never managed to find happiness.

Men who weren't interested in a meaningful relationship weren't worth the effort. She wondered about her mother. Was she so charmed by Oliver Bolles that she had been willing to overlook his basic lack of loyalty?

Anna gave Alistair her address and he used the voice activation to set the navigation. He couldn't travel to that particular suburb of London often.

"What have you found surprising about your new line of work?"

She thought about it. Everything surprised her. "It's quite different from the financial world. Events Management is much more creative and less male-dominated. I've already had the chance to meet with and get to know many talented women. That didn't happen at Blackly Simonson."

He glanced at her. "Was that one of the reasons you decided to shift careers?"

She considered his question. "I wouldn't have realized it before taking this position. As a math major, I was comfortable being in a male-dominated field, but I'm beginning to enjoy less competition and more open communication."

Alistair slowed down for a light and readjusted her seatbelt. She needed to escape his presence. She found everything about him intriguing. The way he drove, the easy way he made conversation, his laugh and the tight muscles under his dress shirt. She tried to remind herself that he was just a man. And an irritating, demanding one at that. A man who rejected her when he realized who she was.

He pulled up to her building and shut off the engine.

"I'm surprised you live in this neighborhood, given your previous salary and the trust fund you must have access to."

His comments about money offended her, but she decided to answer them anyway. "My mother is the one who received a settlement from my father, not me. I wasn't that important to him. My grandparents put aside a set amount for any grandchild that I'll inherit at thirty or when I marry."

"How long have you lived here?"

She undid her seatbelt. "I moved into this neighborhood only a few weeks ago when I resigned from Blackly Simonson. I knew that the salary would be low for a year or two and I would need to be frugal." She didn't like having to explain herself, but it was far better than having him hold onto misconceptions about her.

"Maybe you should have chosen a neighborhood that was more familiar to you."

She met his gaze and opted for complete honesty. "I'm not hooked on material items. I'd rather live within my means."

His eyes narrowed. "Do you worry about crime in this area?"

"I'm tougher than I look." She reached for the door handle.

"Anna." His hand touched hers and her awareness

of him amplified. Being trapped inside the SUV with him was overpowering and intoxicating.

He softened his voice. "We need to talk about what happened between us years ago."

She held back a gasp. "It was nothing." She had no interest in discussing the past.

He touched her chin and forced her to meet his gaze. "I hadn't meant to kiss you so passionately. Somehow, it got out of hand in a flash. I hadn't realized how young you were."

She bristled at his assertion. "I'm not that much younger than you. Maybe six or seven years."

He gently caressed her face. "You weren't yet eighteen and I was twenty-five and only interested in one thing."

She pushed his hand away and picked up her handbag. "I should go."

He cupped her head in his hands. "I want to taste the grown-up you."

She met his gaze and the seriousness of his expression made her stop. Nothing good would come of kissing him.

Alistair leaned forward and kissed her. His strong hands pulled her closer while his tongue sought entrance to her mouth.

She could hear herself sigh and she opened fully to his exploration. He kissed her deeply before pulling back and gently running his fingers over her cheek. He kissed her again. Her desire for him spread throughout her body.

Cradling her head in his hands, Alistair used his mouth to seek a more intimate connection. She was lost in the sensation and reached out to explore his shoulders and chest with her hands.

When she needed a breath, she broke off the kiss and he moved his exploration to her neck. His hand moved down and touched her breast through her shirt, molding his hand to her shape and then flicking his thumb across the sensitive peak. She could feel her nerve endings come alive and she pushed him away.

"We can't do this."

He laughed softly. "We can. I'd like to take you straight to my bed."

She shook her head. "It's impossible. I'm working for you at the moment. I need to go." She straightened her shirt and opened the door.

Climbing out, she didn't let herself look at him. He was too sexy and too intriguing. She needed to block him. Block his wit, charm, and the way he got under her skin. Alistair Martin would break her heart if given the chance. She needed to be smarter than that. He held the keys to unlock the potential of Gala & More with his promise of funding. But how could she accept his offer without getting personally involved with him? It'd be so easy to fall into his bed, but it would ultimately destroy her. Throughout the last several years, she had observed Alistair with a constant string of new romantic partners. He wasn't a good choice. He was like her father. Willing to have a series of relationships, but it would mean nothing.

Chapter 3

By Saturday evening, Anna could feel the tension building in her stomach. She had spent the day overseeing two non-stop events and the last thing she wanted to do was go to Alistair's gala tonight. She hadn't seen him since he kissed her after driving her home.

Rushing around, she took a two-minute shower without getting her hair wet. Stepping out of the bathroom in her tiny flat, she groaned when she glanced at the clock. His event started two hours ago.

The evening dress she borrowed from Olivia hung in the protective sleeve in her closet. It was probably the most valuable item in her flat. Finding sheer stockings, her favorite silver heels and a bra, she dressed. After applying a sweep of makeup, Anna arranged her hair in a neat updo. The fitted and embellished subtle pink dress was shorter than she expected. Without worrying about it, she gathered her keys and handbag and left her building.

Approaching her Zipcar, she glanced inside at the event odds and ends. The afternoon event had been a formal tea at a public library, and all sorts of items needed to be delivered and taken back. A lorry would have been more helpful, instead of packing the car to the brim. She hadn't thought about the day-to-day movement of flowers, rented dishes, decorations, and other items. Frances had promised the job at a discounted rate and she didn't have the heart to cancel it.

She decided not to worry about the car appearing as if she were living out of it. If she attempted to unload it at the office, she wouldn't make the event. At least the Zipcar had navigation. Relaxing somewhat, she thought about the evening ahead. Alistair wanted her to get a sense of the type of gala he put on.

After a thirty-five minute drive from London, his mansion came into view. It gave the impression of an historic castle. Professional valets were parking cars on the enormous lawns of the estate. The sweeping lawns and gardens were beautifully illuminated, with lighting in the trees, along the pathways, and countless ornate hanging lanterns.

Pulling into the circular driveway, a valet stepped forward and opened her car door. The young man didn't show any reaction to her packed hired car. Walking up the stone pathway to the decorated entranceway, she took in a deep breath. A servant greeted her and opened the front door from the outside, and she stepped into the event in full swing.

The formal spaces had enormous displays of flowers, and waiters were circulating with trays of hors d'oeuvres. The French doors on the far wall were opened to the gardens and guests had spilled outside.

The scale of the event impressed her. They were expecting to raise five million pounds for disadvantaged youth tonight. Olivia had told her that each person attending the event had paid five thousand pounds, and then there was a silent auction and a list of benefactors.

Anna glanced through the silent auction items and was intrigued by the experiences and luxury villas donated. There was the use of a yacht on the Mediterranean, a year's worth of wine, a penthouse in New York for a weekend shopping excursion. Someone had put a huge amount of effort into finding unique experiences that would appeal to the wealthy.

She saw Alistair join her and turned slightly to acknowledge him. He was standing close and his subtle masculine scent of rosewood reminded her of his seductive kisses. She had thought about little else in the last week.

His voice was smooth and controlled. "Does anything catch your interest?"

Attempting to clear her thoughts, she said, "Yes. All of it. Whoever put this together was a genius."

Alistair smiled broadly and she realized he had put together the silent auction items. He lightly touched her lower back. "Maybe by the end of the evening, I'll earn your complete adoration."

She put some space between them. "You spent time asking for donations?"

He met her gaze. "As the organizer, I had to stay involved. My marketing team did the displays and the write-ups, but I did the brainstorming and outreach. It's hard to say no to me."

Anna turned to look at the next exhibit. She didn't know how to respond to a flirtatious Alistair. It'd be better to leave their association on a professional footing.

***

He watched her beautiful body hovering as she read the details of a guided hike to Mount Olympus. She wore sexy heels that brought her up to his shoulder and her dress was a layered transparent silk design. Her hair was up, and from behind, he admired her translucent skin and beautifully sculpted arms. Anna tugged at his senses and he was finding it hard to rein in his thoughts.

She turned and smiled at him. "It's all very intriguing."

"Come with me and I'll take you through the hidden areas."

He led her to a busy kitchen where the caterers had taken over and several prep areas were in motion. He introduced her to a few of his staff.

She needed to see the event in action. Every aspect of it had been discussed and orchestrated. His event manager, Simon, was speaking into a headset, reminding the valets to be careful when marking each set of keys. Next, he alerted a wait staff to clean up a spill in the dining room. He was using cameras to watch the formal areas and make sure things were progressing smoothly. Nodding to her and Alistair, he kept up a steady stream of instructions to the staff.

Alistair wanted the evening to be over. The funds raised would exceed expectations, but now he wished the guests would go home. He needed the physical release that only exercise would bring and a tepid shower to cool his passionate thoughts.

Anna seemed to be taking in all the elements. He led her back to the foyer and introduced her to Marcy, who was coordinating the pledges. She stood behind a table in an alcove with a large book and elaborate cash box. He interrupted the couple recording their donation in the book and introduced Anna. The man was in financial services and recognized her as Oliver Bolles's daughter.

Alistair watched as she politely deflected questions about her father. It must be difficult for her. She couldn't possibly have known him well. She was young when Oliver died in the tragic motorcycle accident.

Anna was an odd mixture of the Bolles lineage, but with a much different approach to life. Living in a sketchy neighborhood to pursue her dreams and not asking her family for help. Her father would never have sacrificed his material comforts to pursue a new venture. Oliver Bolles was from old money and sought out luxury and pleasure.

"I'll leave you in Marcy's capable hands for a few minutes while I say hello to a few people."

***

Anna introduced herself to Marcy when the couple drifted away. She explained that she was a partner in a small events management firm that Alistair was considering hiring for a future event. She decided not to mention the possible investment. She wasn't sure what he wanted her to tell his staff.

Marcy spent a few minutes explaining how they secured the pledges. Taking in all of the moving parts, she realized that the attendance created an issue. Most of the formal areas were so crowded that the staff could barely get through with the trays of food.

The rest of the evening flew by. Anna made it a point to speak with the staff and get a sense of the event behind the scenes. Every person she spoke with thought highly of Alistair but worried they weren't working hard enough. He created a culture where everyone understood their role and knew how to conduct themselves. It was a different level of organization and it worried her a little. She liked to give others the freedom to decide how to accomplish their tasks. Alistair seemed to leave very little to chance.

Gala & More hired other companies and expected that it would go well. They didn't micromanage. They took it for granted that it would work out. Maybe she needed to pay more attention and not count on luck.

She caught glimpses of Alistair over the next hour. She had sought out Olivia and Fionn and they introduced her to many of their friends and acquaintances. Many of the people were surprised by her career shift. The women congratulated her, but the men held off giving an opinion.

Anna pushed herself to make conversation and connect with others. She thought back to her time at Blackly Simonson and realized she didn't miss anything about her former life. Except maybe her flat. Her new flat was tiny and run-down. But she was proud of herself for deciding on a different path. She was no longer obsessed with honoring the memory of her father by following in his footsteps. She may have inherited his talent with numbers, but she could choose to lead a different life.

She caught sight of Alistair across the room and her body heated. He was sexy and intriguing. She thought about her teenage crush on him. Taking a sip of champagne, she made herself focus on the fashion conversation happening around her.

Olivia whispered to her, "You spent quite a bit of time with Alistair this evening."

Anna looked at her sister and said in a low voice, "He's considering investing in Gala & More. It's such a coincidence, but when I had that pitch session, he was one of the investors."

Olivia smiled at her. "So he dragged you to this event?" Anna had been so consumed with her new job with little time for anything else, that she hadn't shared the latest news with her sister.

Getting Olivia off by herself for a moment, she said, "He's giving Gala & More an event to plan, so this was a good opportunity to see what his expectations are. I'm a little worried."

"Me too." Olivia widened her eyes and both of them dissolved into laughter.

Fionn interrupted and suggested to Olivia that they head home. Their youngest was having nightmares and they'd promised to be home early.

Fionn gave her a hug and said, "Be careful, Anna. He's not the man for you. He's in another league altogether."

She lowered her head and wondered why Fionn would choose to warn her about Alistair. Was she that transparent?

Olivia whispered, "Just be careful. Fionn is worried that Alistair doesn't take personal relationships seriously. He does seem to move from one woman to another."

Anna kissed her sister on the cheek. "I'm not interested in a fling, so you don't need to worry."

Deciding to seek out Alistair to say goodnight, she glanced through the formal spaces. It was nearly eleven, and she needed a few hours of sleep before she threw herself into a gardening club event in the morning and a book signing the next evening.

He was deep in conversation with an older man, but drew her into the interaction. He then politely excused himself, saying, "I need to show Anna something before she leaves."

He led her to the back of the house and down an elaborate wooden staircase to a stone wine cellar.

The hand-placed stones and old beams reminded her of walking back in time. Glancing around the space, she saw it was neatly kept and massive. The stone walls were impressive and secured wooden racks with wine bottles separated by year and vintage.

"For the celebration, I want to replicate the feel of coming down here. For wine enthusiasts, the wine cellar represents history, success, and abundance. The feeling is pure bliss. I want you to find a venue that replicates this feeling."

Anna glanced around the cellar. It was going to be nearly impossible to replicate a feeling. Not everyone would have the same response. "I imagine it must feel like stepping back in time?"

He watched her closely. "Not exactly. It should be a venue that taps into the feeling of the success that comes with producing a good wine."

She moved further into the wine cellar. "I get that successful events are much more than just combining the right elements. But translating a feeling of pure bliss into an experience for two hundred guests seems impossible."

He stood watching her. "Are you not up to the challenge?"

Anna turned away from him. He was asking far too much, and if she didn't get it right, he would choose not to offer the funding.

"I'll need a few days." She looked at the displayed wine and his organization impressed her. Everything was exact and symmetrical. She had barely reconfigured Gala & More's office space. Worry permeated every bone of her body. She would need to find a way forward.

She met his gaze and attraction sparked between them. He ran a hand through his short hair. The brief kiss a few days ago in the car only served to make her more aware of him. His formal suit concealed a strong, tight body and she wanted to run her hands down his sculpted chest.

She crossed her arms. "I'm intrigued by the challenge, but I need to take care of a few projects first."

He stepped closer to her. "Is Gala & More taking on more work than you can handle?"

Facing him, she said, "Possibly. But that's how we hope to grow."

He crossed his arms. "Be careful. Reputation is crucial at this point. Each event needs to be impressive, stellar."

She leaned back against the cool wall and closed her eyes briefly. She couldn't handle the chemistry between them. Instead of contemplating her next business move, she could only think about throwing herself into his arms.

She opened her eyes and could see desire written in every line of his body. He wanted her and it didn't seem to matter that he was thinking about investing into her company or that they had a social connection through Olivia and Fionn.

Alistair moved forward and captured her mouth. She let out a moan and her hands grasped his tuxedo jacket, pulling him closer. Kissing him back, she matched each stroke of his tongue with her own exploration of his mouth. His hands moved to her hips and he pulled her against him.

She could feel his strength and steadfast focus and wanted to give in to the seduction of it, but held back. He kissed her neck and his tongue lingered on each tender spot. Her breathing sounded ragged to her own ears. When she took in a deep breath, his hands moved to her breasts and desire burned through her.

"We have to stop." She pushed against him.

"Why?" His eyes trailed over her body, consumed with desire.

Why wasn't their business relationship an issue for him? "You have two hundred guests upstairs and my company is asking you for funding. It crosses all sorts of professional and ethical boundaries."

"Sex is merely physical, and doesn't need to affect our professional association. We can feel free to enjoy ourselves and then move on."

He was okay having sex with her tonight and then moving forward in a business relationship tomorrow? Anna shook her head. "I can't do that. That's not how I conduct myself. I can't separate the two. It's getting to the point where I'll have to resign from Gala & More or look for another investor."

***

He found her impossibly sexy. Touching her intricate gown, he wanted to yank the zipper down and expose her beautiful body. If she were willing to let her guard down, he'd tempt her upstairs to his bedroom, but she was going to require more patience. They should take care of the business aspects before indulging in more physical pleasures. "We can keep our association strictly professional until the deal is finished. Does that work?"

Her flushed skin and her tongue darting out to moisten her lips told him that she felt desire for him. He could barely rein in his physical response and moved away from her as she said, "Yes. I can't think properly with the attraction between us."

A slow smile spread across his face. "I'm not sure if you should admit that. It gives me the advantage." He straightened his jacket.

A flurry of emotions crossed over her face. He surprised her with his admission. But, in some ways, that would help them keep a reasonable distance until a decision was made. He was complicating the entire scenario for himself and breaking his own rules to have her. He believed in keeping business and his personal life separate. It was one of the reasons he stopped seeing Brenda Waterman.

Her expression was downcast and Alistair wanted to see her smile, but he held back.

"I shouldn't keep you from your guests. I'll see you Tuesday?"

He smiled at her. "Yes. The reveal for the streamlined Gala office."

Following her up the stairs, his desire skyrocketed watching her long, shapely legs navigate each step.

The deal couldn't be signed soon enough. They

weren't asking for too much investment and they had the talent and the contacts to grow the business. It was a no-brainer for him, but for some reason he wanted to have an inside view of her building the company. He didn't want to give them funding and walk away. He wanted to see how she would grow and expand the company.

He walked with her to the entrance foyer and said, "Goodnight, Anna."

For a brief moment, he considered kissing her on the mouth without a care for what his guests thought, but he decided to respect her boundaries and smiled at her instead.

She responded only with, "Thank you for inviting me."

***

Turning away from him, Anna reminded herself to breathe. The atmosphere in the wine cellar remained with her. He was immensely attractive, and at the same time she worried if she could handle the professional pressure. How could she possibly come up with a celebration that would please him? His expectations were insane. The guests would expect a tremendous amount from an Alistair Martin event. Not only did everyone who was invited attend, but many of the guests also asked to bring others. His event coordinator had to turn people away.

Waiting for her car to be brought up, she thought about him. He confused her. His castle was modernized yet authentic, and marvelously maintained with formal gardens, elaborate furnishings, and all of the modern conveniences. But why would a single man choose to live on a country estate instead of in

London?

The valet handed her keys to her Zipcar and she barely registered him. How would she find the perfect setting? How would she hold him off until the deal was finished? If he rejected the business deal, would she be just as enamored of him? Her body didn't care if he rejected the deal or not. But was it wise to agree to leap into an affair with him? He wasn't interested in any type of permanence. Or, maybe she needed to let go of her worries and enjoy herself instead of considering the future.

Driving home, her mind tried to make sense of the evening, but for some reason she kept thinking about her desire for him. If she were being practical, she would sprint in the opposite direction. But she didn't want to run away. She wanted to see how everything would work out, even if it meant that things ended badly between them.

Chapter 4

Walking into the revamped office space on Tuesday morning, Anna relaxed slightly. She had bought flowers and plants that morning and then retrieved a few lamps and pieces of artwork from her storage unit to decorate the empty space.

Anna had rescheduled a day of appointments and worked long hours between Sunday and Monday, along with Elyse and Katie, to transform the office. They hired a handyman to keep removing trash, odd items, and other unwanted paraphernalia throughout the two days. They had also coaxed him into helping them move the furniture into a new configuration.

She and Katie had gotten rid of the makeshift eating area and decided to order out for coffee when they needed it. She hired a cleaning crew to steam clean the carpets and wash the walls, woodwork, and windows that evening. She would hire a painter to fix the ceiling next week.

She spent time arranging the plants and flowers and then hanging the artwork.

Arriving just after ten o'clock, Katie and Elyse came in with coffee and pastries. The three of them spent a few minutes looking around the space.

Elyse pointed at the floor. "I didn't know the

carpet was an off white. I thought it was brown."

"Having art on the walls gives the space a more finished look." Anna gazed at the pieces that had been in her previous flat. Most of them were bright, modern paintings. But it worked.

Katie asked, "What is Mr. Martin looking for?"

"He wants to see Gala & More in action. So relax and go about your normal routine."

They looked at her blankly. She explained, "Answer incoming calls, reach out to clients, and do research on the internet."

Elyse said, "I don't know where anything is now. It was a disaster before, but I could find things."

Anna made an effort not to roll her eyes. "We put the client files inside the desks along with all the office supplies. Just sit at your revamped workspace and see if you can establish a routine."

Katie and Elyse took their coffee to their desks and began to pull out files and turn on their computers.

"So when is our hot new investor arriving?" Elyse asked.

Anna crossed her arms and said, "I don't think you should refer to him in that manner. He is a professional and we are lucky he's considering a large investment into Gala & More."

"Anna, he's gorgeous. I don't know how you think about business when you're with him," Katie chimed in.

Anna fidgeted with her necklace. There was no way she was going to tell them that she was contemplating having a wild fling with him. She would need to be discreet. She had no interest in being the center of gossip. "It's important to keep any interaction on a professional level."

"Really?" Katie questioned her.

She rolled her eyes. "Never mind. Let's get started with our day."

Opening her laptop on the conference room table, Anna began to organize her thoughts. She had considered different venues for the Martin event while she had been cleaning out and organizing the office. Taking out a pen, she began jotting down a few ideas.

At eleven o'clock, Alistair rang the buzzer. She saw him through the front window and pulled open the door.

"So, what they say about you is true. You're a bit of a miracle worker." His voice sounded warm and intimate. For a split second, she thought he would kiss her.

"Good morning. Please come in."

Katie and Elyse came forward. Anna introduced them to Alistair.

He smiled and shook each of their hands. "It's lovely to meet both of you. I've been to some fabulous events organized by Gala & More."

After a few minutes of small talk, Katie and Elyse went back to work and Anna brought him to the conference room. After hesitating briefly, she closed the door.

Alistair took a seat opposite her. "Do you bring clients here?"

"You are the first, I believe."

"You may want to consider a white board and project management visuals or photographs of events you have managed. The artwork is nice but is more suitable to a luxury flat."

She put her pen down. He must know she had spent every spare moment getting ready for his visit.

"I'll take that under consideration. Maybe we should discuss your event."

He leaned back in his chair. "Tsk. Tsk. Remember, I'm not just a client but your potential investor."

Her hands clenched briefly. He could be infuriating. She made an effort to relax and said, "Gala & More could survive without your funding. It may take longer to build and expand, but I feel the need to inform you that I'm not interested in your business advice."

Alistair stood up and moved to the window. "Be careful. If you're not interested in my business advice, then I don't know how this deal could move forward."

Why did he have to be so impossible? He had built an empire, but not in event management. Running a vineyard and managing a slew of breweries was completely different from an event management company.

She needed to backtrack. "I'm not saying that I'm unwilling to hear constructive criticism."

A quiet settled over the space. She met his gaze and Katie's earlier words came back to her. It was hard to concentrate with the sparks flying between them. He was captivating and intriguing in equal measure.

"Gala & More has some redeeming traits. The clients have raved about the service. But the internal business practices need improving. You would be smart to take some advice."

"I'm open to new ideas for improving the

company." Her voice was neutral and calm.

"But not from me?" Alistair leaned against the wall.

She placed both of her hands on the conference room table and stood up. "You must realize I've spent the last forty-eight hours reinventing this space. I've barely taken a breath. Instead of acknowledging the progress, you are looking for new hurdles for me to jump through."

He sat down again and leaned back in his chair. "If you intend to build a business worthy of investment, you need to keep pushing forward. It's not enough to get to a comfortable place. If you want success, you have to keep challenging yourself."

She needed to stop resisting and allow herself to take criticism. She was used to knowing everything and working without oversight. Having to consider ideas from Frances, the staff, and now Alistair was too much. Maybe she didn't like collaboration as much as she had thought.

She took a calming breath and settled back into her chair. "Agreed. I have a few ideas for the wine launch and would love your feedback."

Alistair met her gaze. "I'm all yours for another hour."

She would love an hour with him, but made herself banish the provocative thought. Instead, she pulled up his client file and turned her laptop towards him.

Anna picked up the remote to advance the slides and began pacing the room. It would have been easier to wear flats, but her heels were comfortable. Her pencil skirt and tailored silk shirt kept her body in an elegant line.

"I'd love to find a venue tied into the wine industry. But, it's tricky to bring two hundred guests to a working vineyard. I've found a few public gardens with extensive grape vines and all the amenities needed to host a large event."

She clicked through various slides showing public gardens and open spaces near London.

Alistair frowned. "Your concept is to use a public garden to host the event?"

Her heart raced and she took in a deep breath to slow her response. "Yes. I realize there will be some complications. The public gardens have ample parking, modern bathrooms and access to water and electricity. There are a dozen or so gardens within driving distance from London. I'll visit each one and narrow down the selection to the best two or three."

"Martin Enterprises typically makes use of one of our breweries or a luxury hotel for a launch."

She kept her voice neutral. "This would be a departure from the normal event, but it would create interest and excitement. Many of your guests have been to the same event countless times."

He crossed his arms. "I like your concept, but there would be complications to manage."

Anna continued to pace. "Another selling point is that many of the public gardens are in desperate need of funds. By hosting your event there, you would be creating positive buzz by giving back."

"It needs to have the feel of a vineyard." He checked the time on his phone.

"Absolutely. I'm looking for the right space. When would you like to meet again?" Anna turned her laptop away from him and accessed her calendar.

He watched her closely. "I've blocked off the next few Wednesdays at four o'clock, if that works for you?"

She nodded. "Perfect."

"I've had a chance to look over your financials and have a few thoughts."

Glancing at him, she could only imagine what he would say. Frances didn't have a head for numbers and their accounts were in poor shape. Vendors hadn't been paid, and many clients were late paying their bills to Gala & More. Frances didn't go back and charge for add-on services, causing many of the events they managed to lose money. She was beginning to see that Frances was a pushover and clients knew it.

Anna tapped her pen on her notepad, looking down at it. Whenever she glanced at him, her mind would lose focus. "I've been analyzing the financials and adjusting the contractual process."

He said, "In working through the financials, you'll have to be careful not to disrupt your central selling proposition. Gala & More has been drawing clients in and you wouldn't want to adversely affect that."

Anna sat back down. "Being the low bidder has an impact on the bottom line. Gala & More will either need to pull back on offering so much or charge more. In a small shift, I've developed a process to charge for add-ons and I'm insisting on a higher deposit."

"Those adjustments will help. You'll also need to find a better location for your offices."

She shook her head. "We can't move without a substantial investment."

Alistair stood. "I'd like you to visit Martin Wineries next week for a couple of days."

Why would he want her to? She had so much work to do. "As a day trip?" The vineyard was a few hours by train.

"Seeing the operations firsthand will give you a better sense of the business. I'm heading down there next Wednesday afternoon through Friday, and would like you to come with me."

Her mind went into overdrive. It had to be business. He couldn't be suggesting a romantic getaway. They had agreed to wait.

"It's difficult to take time off."

He smiled at her. "It's not really taking time off. I imagine your most important client is Martin Wineries."

She needed his investment. How difficult could it be to walk around a vineyard? "I'll clear my schedule." Anna stood and held her hand out to him.

Alistair reached forward and enfolded her hand in a warm caress. She could feel her body begin to heat and stepped back.

"Thank you for coming." She walked him to the door and took a deep breath as he left.

Katie and Elyse followed her back into the conference room.

"Did it go well?" Katie asked.

Anna took a sip of her cold coffee and made a funny face. "We're still in the running."

"He's a catch for some lucky girl. His stamina must be off the charts," Elyse said.

Katie laughed. "I wouldn't mind trying him out."

Anna threw away her cup. "Keep in mind, he's a

client and you are both happily married."

Elyse said, "He's drop-dead gorgeous. How can you spend time with him and not incinerate?"

Anna decided to keep her feelings to herself. In the end, it was impossible to predict how everything would turn out. "He has a keen intellect and asks tough questions. It'd not serve Gala & More well if I lost my head."

"So you haven't noticed how hot he is?" Katie raised her eyebrows.

"I met him years ago. His close friend is married to my sister, so I've seen him occasionally at social gatherings."

"I hope he decides that Gala & More is worth the investment," Katie said.

Anna looked out the window. "It won't be easy. He has many hurdles for us to jump over. We have to be careful quoting new projects and make sure each one comes in on budget. He also wants less artwork and more business stuff."

"This place is so much improved, but we could use a white board and photographs of different venues we recommend," Elyse suggested.

"I agree. But, we may want to rent a different space first. Closer to the business district."

"If we spend more on rent, won't that impact the bottom line?" Katie's husband was looking for work and she had a nine-month-old son.

Anna straightened the files on the table. "Yes and no. This space can't be used for client meetings. Most clients would worry about parking their car. We have been getting hired in spite of it. And think about how nice it would be to be closer to some of the rental places, florists, and hotels."

They spent the next few hours strategizing about upcoming events and creating task lists. Anna relaxed as she realized that Katie and Elyse were both competent and resourceful. On a positive note, the tiring work of cleaning out the office had made them more of a team.

She hadn't wanted to worry Frances, but their business account was nearly empty. Anna would need to take money out of her dwindling savings to cover their payroll for the next month and forgo a paycheck for herself. Hopefully, they would finalize the investment deal with Alistair so she wouldn't need to go through all her reserves.

What else would he require of her before he agreed to invest in Gala & More? She immersed herself in research for his wine launch, trying not to obsess about the future.

***

By the following Wednesday, Anna had worked twenty-seven straight days. Reminding herself that failure was not an option, she packed an overnight bag for her trip to the Martin Wineries. Heading into the office, she mentally reviewed her schedule again. Gala & More had numerous events to plan and the cash flow had improved slightly.

Stepping into the office, she saw that Katie and Elyse were already at their desks. They would have to handle the last minute details of a fiftieth birthday celebration for a well-known CEO while she headed to the vineyard.

She set up her laptop on the conference room table and replied to her emails. Looking at her schedule, she saw they didn't have an event for Sunday, so she sent a text message to Olivia offering to spend time with her nieces.

By the afternoon, she gave up on work after she glanced at the clock for a second time in a few minutes. Why had Alistair asked her to accompany him to the vineyard? He had an intensity that put her on guard, and now she was at a disadvantage, waiting for him to decide whether or not to fund the company. She was in over her head. The frequent calls to Frances helped somewhat, but she had been thrown into a chaotic, disorganized mess.

Alistair texted her at precisely three o'clock letting her know he was outside. She wished Katie and Elyse luck with the next few days and gathered her laptop and overnight bag. Leaving the office, she noticed him a block and a half away leaning against his shiny red Land Rover.

***

He watched the reserved Ms. Bolles balance her overnight case, laptop, and handbag. Their family connection complicated things. He had met her father on several occasions, and was unimpressed with his lack of integrity and despised his pettiness. Supposedly, Anna Bolles was his prodigy. She had inherited his mathematical mind and cool façade, and the English heredity was obvious in her bone structure and blond hair. But, she didn't remind him of Oliver at all. She was far more independent and cared about others.

Why was he even bothering with a possible investment? He should tell her no and be done with it. But something held him back. It couldn't be the past;

he didn't harbor ill will towards a deceased, fallen-from-grace icon. Or did he? Oliver had been cruel to him on a few occasions and openly declared that he would fail in the wine business. Maybe his motives weren't altogether altruistic?

He shook his head and banished the negative thoughts. Alistair had proven the old man wrong and was on hand when Fionn publically split from him. In the end, Oliver was a defeated man, even if he had pretended otherwise.

Anna stood in front of him and he could see the unmistakable challenge in her gaze.

"Ms. Bolles." He smiled at her. "Are you ready?"

He opened the door for her, taking her suitcase and laptop bag to stow in the back. She climbed into the passenger seat, put on her sunglasses and remained quiet.

She untangled her hair from the seatbelt. "How long will the drive take?" Wearing the dark glasses, he couldn't tell what she was thinking.

Alistair started the vehicle. "It depends on traffic. Three hours is typical."

She turned towards him. "I'm zonked and I've been known to sleep on long drives."

He glanced at her. "You'll have to tell me what has kept you so busy. That is, until you fall asleep." For some inexplicable reason, he wanted to get a reaction from her.

***

Anna took in a calming breath. Why did Alistair Martin have to appoint himself their business advisor? It was tough enough trying to learn the business without someone looking over her shoulder and questioning every decision.

She turned her phone to silent and slipped it into her handbag. "We should set some ground rules for the discussions."

"I'm not much of a rule follower." He looked at her and his stare lingered for a moment, causing her body to heat.

Why did every conversation have to be fraught with sexual undertones? "Well…you'll find that I'm a rule follower."

Alistair pulled into traffic. "If you intend to lead a company, you may want to rethink your approach."

"A business also needs structure and sound processes. The issue I've had with Gala & More is that it seems to be all out-of-the-box thinking."

He shifted gears. "Be careful. I'm both your client and potential investor. Don't give me a reason not to hire or invest in Gala & More."

He was impossible. Anna took off her sunglasses and looked at him. "Exactly how can you be both an advisor and a potential client? There are inherent conflicts."

"That falls to you to manage the expectations. You're in a tricky position. You need to both impress me and be willing to take guidance." His voice held a slightly teasing note.

Anna looked out of the window. Why did he have to be so difficult? She didn't want to spend three days sparring with him. She preferred to live a solitary existence and be able to plan things out. It had to do with her father. He'd pop into her life when it was convenient for him, bringing sunshine and magic, and then would arbitrarily leave. She needed to avoid getting involved with him. Eventually, she needed someone who was steady and predictable, not someone like her father. Larger than life, embracing new ideas, and ready for an adventure. Alistair Martin was not a safe choice for her.

She put her sunglasses back in place and looked straight ahead. "Why are you willing to give Gala & More your time? You must be extremely busy running Martin Wineries."

He glanced at her briefly before focusing on the traffic. "It's not much of a time commitment and it's a challenge. If Gala & More finds a logical way to expand, then it would add to my portfolio, possibly breathe new life into a product launch, and satisfy my entrepreneurial spirit."

She thought about his reasons. Fionn had told her that he'd had no connection to the Martin family until he was a teenager. Alistair was a self-made man. So why did he push himself so hard? "Isn't running your business empire enough? Fionn said you have expanded your holdings tenfold in the last decade."

He kept his focus on the road. "It's thriving and making tons of profit, but the challenge is gone. I'm looking for new ventures. That's what drew me to the investment network. I've invested in three start-ups in the last year."

She glanced at his stark profile. "What if the businesses fail?"

He shrugged. "I never invest more than I can easily afford to lose. Not every business will succeed. I seek out new opportunities that present a challenge but have massive potential."

***

Alistair decided not to disclose too much. Truth be told, he had considered walking away from Gala & More. The principal owner was creatively brilliant, but her financials were a train wreck. If she hadn't enticed Anna to join her, he wouldn't have looked seriously at the company. He'd have walked away—or even sprinted. But, he liked Anna's willingness to fight, and she had the financial ability to stabilize the company. She may be in over her head, but she was willing to roll up her sleeves and work harder.

He intended to test her resolve over the next couple of days. Would she be willing to throw herself into the work at the vineyard, or would she sit back and wait for him to spoon-feed her the information?

Anna took a sip from her water bottle. "Do you have any family members involved in the business?"

He invited her to the vineyard to get to know her, not to delve into family history. "No. I was an only child and so was my father. My grandparents are alive and well, but they're in their eighties."

"Is it hard to work under your father's shadow?"

Fionn must have shared the basics of his upbringing. His mother struggled in a service job while he ran wild on the streets of Dublin. His childhood was never far from his thoughts. His chest tightened. "No. He wasn't involved in the business. He refused any connection to me, but when he died, my grandfather came and pleaded with my mother to allow him to provide for my education. I was fifteen and up to no good, so he convinced my mom to relocate to the UK and put me in an elite boarding school."

Anna touched her pendant, a mannerism he was

beginning to recognize that meant she was deep in thought.

"That must have been quite a culture shock."

He thought about the early fights with his classmates and the kindness of his grandmother. She had insisted that he wasn't so different and set out to polish his rough edges. But he was different. If his wealth disappeared overnight, he'd survive. He was more comfortable in the poverty-stricken public housing than he would ever be in the mansions and exclusive vacation destinations that the wealthy sought out.

Anna Bolles was from the elite world of private school education, skiing in the Alps, and living with servants. She had chosen to live in a working-class neighborhood but it was still different from the slums he grew up in.

He ran a hand through his hair. "My academic achievements saved me. I scored in the top few spots each semester, so the teachers would find ways to deal with my behavior."

"Did you miss home while at boarding school?"

He could feel her watching him, but he didn't turn to look at her. "My grandfather arranged for my mother to be offered a job and an apartment on campus, so I saw her most days, and on the weekends I stayed with her."

Anna took another sip of water. "My experience was quite different. I went to a large boarding school and was lucky to see my mother twice a year."

He watched her rub her hands along her upper arms. Was she trying to protect herself from the memories? He didn't want to feel empathy for her. He needed to decide on the investment and not get involved emotionally.

***

They lapsed into silence and Anna could feel herself drifting off to sleep. She had been working twenty-hour days and it was catching up with her. Alistair turned on a classic opera and sleep overtook her.

The vehicle maneuvered sharply to the right and Anna came out of a deep sleep. It took a moment to get her bearings.

"Are we at Martin Wineries?" She attempted to sound coherent.

"Yes, you've been dead to the world for the last two hours."

Stretching in her seat, she tried to push away a feeling of awkwardness. What if she mumbled something odd in her sleep? A habit her college roommates teased her about. She needed a bathroom and some coffee.

Alistair pulled into a circular courtyard and parked in front of a large field stone mansion. Getting out, he walked around to the back of the vehicle and opened the boot to retrieve their luggage.

She opened the door and admired the beautiful landscaping. Her legs were not completely steady, but she stretched and walked slowly towards Alistair.

"You're not fully awake yet."

She took her laptop case from him. "No. I'm still sleepy."

Alistair led her up to the front door and opened it. Stepping inside, she took in the rustic charm of the house.

"Do your grandparents live here?"

He turned to her. "They lived most of their married life here. Now they have a modern, smaller residence on the other side of the vineyard overlooking a lake. I turned this mansion into a guest house for the vineyard and we host several events a year here."

A housekeeper greeted them and offered to help her with the bags. Alistair told her he would see her on the terrace in an hour for dinner.

The efficient housekeeper showed her to a guest suite on the second floor and explained how to find the terrace.

"Do you have any food allergies I should let the cook know about?"

She shook her head. "I'm fine with anything."

The woman smiled and left the room. Anna looked out the old-fashioned windows and could see acres and acres of vines on the rolling hills. The sun cast a magnificent haze over the entire valley.

Finding her phone, she took several photographs and texted a few to Katie and Elyse. Katie asked how the drive went with Alistair. She responded that she had fallen asleep.

Her assistant's obsession with Alistair's hotness was beginning to bother her. It was even more annoying that he seemed to know that the opposite sex found him irresistible.

After reading a text that her nieces had a cold, she sent a message to her sister.

She unpacked and hung up her clothing, then took a long, hot shower to relax. The bathroom was modern and sizeable, and she attempted to silence her worries.

Was she expected to dress for dinner? She had

brought a sleeveless black sheath dress that followed her curves. It fell just above her knee and she added silver, strappy sandals. Deciding to leave her hair loose, she put on a long pendant necklace and carefully applied eyeliner and mascara. She wondered who else might join them.

Her heels clicked on the stone floor when she stepped out onto the terrace. Alistair was on his phone but ended the call. He was dressed in worn jeans and a close fitting black T-shirt. His casual clothing adhered to his perfectly sculpted chest and arms.

He glanced at her dress. "I should have mentioned that we keep it somewhat casual for dinner."

Anna held up her hands. "I didn't know if the dinner would be more proper."

He pulled out a chair for her. "Dinner is usually a casserole with bread and wine."

She was overdressed. Alistair was watching her with a curious look.

"Would you like me to change?"

He smiled and she could feel her heart constrict. "No. You look stunning."

She needed to put some distance between them. She worked for him and had to remember this was all about investing in the company.

The housekeeper had prepared a delicious roast chicken with root vegetables. She served the plates hot and headed inside.

Alistair poured her a glass of wine. "I created this wine. It can't be sold in the UK because it includes grapes from Costa Rica."

"I didn't realize that there's a restriction on imported wine."

He took a sip of his wine. "It can be given away. I had a thousand bottles produced. So the idea is to introduce it at the event and then send everyone home with a few bottles."

Anna took a bite of the delicious dinner. She swirled the wine for a moment then took a sip. "I like it. The complex flavor enhances the meal."

Alistair took a bite of his meal. "Have you always liked wine?"

"I've taken classes in wine tasting. It seemed important to know how to choose an appropriate wine. But in school and even now in the workplace, many men drink lager."

He nodded. "I enjoy lager as well, but slowly I've become a connoisseur of wine."

She watched him across the table. "You have several microbreweries. Were your grandparents resistant to you getting into a separate business?"

He looked relaxed and approachable tonight. "My grandparents knew I hated to be reined in, so they never complained. And it panned out-the business has an insane net worth."

She loved seeing a relaxed side of the hugely popular entrepreneur. "How did you know that you would be successful in the brewery business?"

"I didn't. I took a chance. When I opened the first microbrewery, my grandparents were nervous. But over time, they relaxed and now will even attend events held there."

Anna thought about his grandparents and how they must be so proud of him.

He took a swallow of his wine and watched her with a hooded gaze. "There's something I can't quite work out about you. You were a math prodigy, attended Oxford, accepted a position at Blackly Simonson, and even had an article about your early success in Vanity Fair. But you walked away and threw yourself into a poorly run start-up. It seems counterintuitive."

Anna let a moment go by and then decided to disclose something about her decision. She hated pretense, so even if it made life difficult, she made an effort to be open and forthcoming with information. "I was living the life others expected of me. I probably would have continued, but something happened and I crossed paths with Frances Casey. After seeing her life, I knew I had to change mine."

"How did your paths cross?" His gazed seared into her.

She wasn't ready for all the questions that would arise, but she also didn't want to hide from the truth. "I'm not sure it's relevant and I don't think you would want to hear the truth."

"The truth is everything, Anna. Try me."

The housekeeper came and cleared away their dishes.

The darkness of the night had descended slowly and Alistair got up and lit a few candles. Light also spilled out of the house, but the shadows gave her the courage to tell him about her past.

"There was a man hired recently at Blackly Simonson that I had gone to school with but I hadn't seen in five years. While we were in college, he had tried to blackmail me over something that had happened. I handled it and refused to give him any money. But a few years later, Frances Casey approached me about an incident with her sister. By not coming forward, I had put other women at risk."

"I'm sorry, Anna."

"There have been other criminal incidents he was involved in and charges filed against him. But each time, he somehow escaped unscathed. He was hired in spite of the allegations. I saw how he was given so much respect for his family connections that I decided I didn't want to be a part of that world any longer."

His voice was quiet. "What world are you taking about?"

She tried to keep the bitterness out of her voice. "Basically the financial world in London and elsewhere is testosterone-driven, competitive, materialistic, and all about results, not people."

He looked perplexed. "This person was someone you had dated?"

She probably shouldn't have set down the path of truth telling. Now he would ask her all sorts of questions.

***

He watched as she crumbled into a deep cavern. How could he possibly reverse this conversation? He didn't need to know the intimate details of her life or the mistakes she had made. He had enough of his own to contend with.

"Anna, I was curious as to why you changed careers. You don't need to share anything that would upset you. But, know that in my thirty years, I've seen way too much. Nothing you say would shock or upset me. We all make choices, sometimes bad ones, about drugs, sexual adventures, and other pursuits."

He watched her nod. Something was wrong. This wasn't about changing careers.

Alistair took a sip of wine. "Why was this man blackmailing you?"

She gripped herself in a tight hold. "I became an easy target when I started using the Bolles name. People think that it opens doors, grants instant respect and such. But there's a dark side. It allows those who want to take advantage and threaten a young woman to have a certain amount of power."

He wasn't following her generalizations, but she looked so powerless and fragile that he didn't want to push her.

Still, he asked, "Did he have a compromising photograph of you or a story?"

"He drugged me when I was nineteen and had one of his friends take a video while he sexually assaulted me."

"He raped you?" He kept his voice neutral but anger surged through his body.

"I have no memory of what actually happened. He sent me short video clips that show him undressing me but not an actual rape."

He leaned forward. "Did you go to the police?"

She shook her head. "Not at first. I went to a clinic, then home to see my mother. He was from a powerful family and she didn't want to file a report."

"But you eventually went to the police?"

She touched her wine glass. "I hired a private detective to find out more about him. He wanted a large sum of money, but I didn't tell my mother because she would have paid it."

He kept his tone light. "Had he done something similar to Frances Casey's sister?"

A few tears slid down her cheeks and she wiped them away. "Three years after my incident, he drugged and assaulted her younger sister. The girl didn't want to press charges, but around that time the private detective put me in touch with Frances."

"Nothing happened to him?"

Her voice wavered. "Charges were filed by someone else. Frances and I had approached the girl and explained the history. It went to trial, but he's smart, powerful, and his family had money and connections. He was acquitted of the charges and his family had him go through an anger management program."

Her quiet strength amazed him. She hadn't allowed herself to use money to buy her way out of the problem. She had been young to deal with the issue all by herself. "Has he approached you recently?"

She shook her head. "No. I saw him at Blackly Simonson, but he pretended not to know me. He has the video somewhere. I've paid private detectives to look for it, but he's too smart for that."

He reached out and placed his hand over hers. "What do you intend to do?"

She sat back. "Nothing. I spent five years trying to seek revenge, but in the end it was just hurting me. I did give the police a statement and agreed to cooperate if it comes to that in the future."

A few moments of silence passed between them.

Anna continued, "He's done this a dozen times. It's how he acquires large sums of money for his other pursuits. The women victimized are all young, from wealthy families, and didn't want to face an embarrassing scandal."

"How is Frances Casey's sister doing?"

She held his gaze. "She joined the Peace Corps and is in India for two years."

Anna was so much more complicated than he expected. "I'm sorry this happened to you. But you were brave to face it and not pay him."

She wiped away a few more tears and stood up. "It's hard to talk about it. It was a very painful time. My father had died and I was completely alone."

He stood up and stepped forward, gathering her in his arms. She stiffened slightly and he let her go. "Anna..."

She stepped further away. "Goodnight, Alistair."

He watched her leave the terrace. She was sensitive and strong at the same time. Now he understood why she had chosen a different path. The fighter in him would not let this go. He would destroy the man. Not in an obvious way, but he would make sure he lost his job and would face a few consequences.

He'd thought she had an easy life being a Bolles prodigy. But she was surprising him at each turn. She hadn't become bitter or destroyed by the incident; instead, it had made her stronger. She had hired a private detective to help find the evidence, and he guessed to prevent the man from doing something similar to other young women. She had taken a risk. If the man suspected, he could have come after her.

With every moment Alistair spent with Anna, he was falling further under her spell. He had been tempted by her physically years ago, but now having the opportunity to see how her mind worked, her willingness to fight for fairness and her capacity for depth, and he was so drawn to her that he didn't want to hold back. He only kept himself in check because he had promised to wait until the decision was made about Gala & More before pursuing a physical relationship. He shouldn't have pursued an investment into her company; instead, he should have pursued her. Now he was stuck waiting for the business to be sorted out before finding any satisfaction.

Alistair craved a connection to her and it scared him. Personal relationships had never been complicated for him. But, somehow Anna Bolles had gotten under his skin, and now he had to decide whether to walk away or indulge his fantasies.

Chapter 5

The next morning, Alistair met Anna at sunrise in the main foyer. She wore slim-fitting jeans and a white T-shirt, and didn't make eye contact with him. She must regret sharing her story last night. He needed a distraction. Spending a few days with Anna wasn't working out as he expected.

"I'm impressed you own a pair of work boots." Physical labor mustn't be as alien to her as he first suspected.

She glanced at him. "I've done a fair amount of gardening, but have very limited experience with grape vines."

Being careful to lower his voice, he asked, "Anna, do you regret telling me about your past?"

Her chin lifted but her eyes held a shadowy regard. "I don't regret telling you, but it's not something I enjoy discussing."

He understood her dilemma. As a rule, he didn't reveal more than was necessary, but her unadorned admission had sparked something deep inside him. "It didn't shock me. If anything, I'm impressed with your resolve and strength."

Crossing her arms, she said, "It's a difficult line to navigate, though. Our connection extends beyond a merely professional association, so I'm not sure how much to share with you."

Alistair nodded. He wanted her to share freely all of her thoughts and ideas, not to hold anything back. Typically, he encouraged others to show restraint and not to share emotional thoughts. Why did he treat her so differently? "Come. I'd like to show you the vineyard before I hand you over to my foreman."

The housekeeper greeted them on the terrace and handed Alistair two thermal coffee cups.

He handed a cup to Anna. "Do you want something to eat before we start the day?"

She shook her head. "Coffee is fine."

He made eye contact with the housekeeper. "Thank you. We won't have breakfast this morning."

He led Anna out into the vineyard. The morning air was cool, but by mid-day it would be hot in the sun.

Walking down the steps, he asked, "Do you need a hat? The sun is intense."

She met his gaze. "You're rather considerate today. I have a scarf and sunscreen in my bag."

Just being with her, he wanted to forget about work, but he said, "I'll give you a quick tour of the vineyard and then I'll assign you to one of the work groups to do pruning and weeding."

He had reconsidered asking her to work on the vines after last night, but his instinct told him that she would enjoy seeing how the grapes were grown. It would ground her in the inner workings of the vineyard and possibly spark an idea for their harvest celebration.

Driving on the dirt roads in an all-terrain vehicle,

he pointed out various aspects of the vineyard. She seemed fascinated by the work and asked several questions. After nearly an hour of exploring the grounds during sunrise, he drove to the work building and introduced her to the staff. His foreman, Bowen Arnold, an older man with thick white hair and an easy laugh, assigned her to a crew for the day.

Alistair worked in the fermentation barn, going over the equipment and making adjustments before heading out to check out the fields. He caught sight of Anna at noon but was kept busy and didn't speak with her.

He was checking a new variation of grape with his foreman when a worker brought her to him at five o'clock.

Anna removed her work gloves and pushed a strand of hair away from her face. "Thank you. I enjoyed working with you."

"You should come back when we harvest. It'll be more interesting." The young man nodded to Bowen and headed back to the barn.

Bowen said to her, "The crew liked having you along. I hope you come again."

Anna reached forward and shook Bowen's hand. "Thank you for welcoming me."

The conversation lasted another few minutes until Alistair became concerned that she would collapse at his feet.

***

Anna stretched her neck gently. Every muscle in her body ached. The day had started out slow and enjoyable, but the further they got into the work, the more she had to struggle to keep pace with the other workers. A ten-kilometer run didn't exhaust her, but today, she garnered a new respect for working at a vineyard. She enjoyed the continuous banter and openness of the team she worked alongside. The best part of the day had been listening to them discuss their busy lives and their families.

Alistair had smudges of rich, dark soil on his chest and had visible scratches on his arm. She thought of him as a CEO and not one who would participate in the daily work of the vineyard. But he was clearly at ease with the workers and understood the internal workings of running the vineyard.

He turned to her. "Why don't we head back to the guest house?"

She nodded, and then turned to Bowen and said, "Thank you. Your crew couldn't have been more helpful and encouraging."

The foreman smiled broadly and said, "I hope you come back."

Alistair said, "Goodnight, Bowen."

Anna followed him and they walked back between the rows of grape vines. She snapped a few close-up photographs of the grape vines with her phone.

He stopped walking and she nearly collided with him. A silence stretched between them and she wondered what he was thinking about.

"I'm finding it hard to concentrate on work with you here."

Anna inwardly winced. "I shouldn't have told you about the incident. I could have just said that I met Frances through a mutual friend. I don't know why I did. It must have something to do with proving that

I'm nothing like my father."

He reached out and gently touched her hand. "I wasn't referring to last night, but your deliberate decision to tell the truth does set you apart from him."

She took a step back and removed her hand. He knew too much about her now. Maybe that was her motivation. Maybe she wanted to scare him off. "It's awkward having you know so much about me. I should have left our association on a more professional basis."

He flexed his shoulders. "Without knowing the background, your choices didn't make sense. I was leaning towards not funding Gala & More on the belief that you would go back to your old life. Now I'm more inclined to take a chance."

Her voice faltered slightly. "I didn't tell you everything to gain your sympathy or pity."

He ran a hand through his hair. "I don't feel sorry for you. You made certain choices. But I do have a deeper understanding of why you made those decisions and why you and Frances have formed a connection." He continued walking to the house.

She was relieved that he didn't feel sorry for her, but could they manage to get to a more professional relationship? She was trying to push aside her growing desire for him, but it was getting more difficult. Sharing her past with him hadn't created distance; instead, it had somehow linked her to him.

They climbed the front steps and he turned to her. "What happens when a man comes on to you? Do you go back to that incident in your mind?"

She stopped and looked at him. Her past hadn't dampened his desire. Instead, he wanted to know how it affected her.

She suppressed a smile. "What happens to you when a woman comes on to you? Do you go back to some negative experience?"

He shrugged. "I don't have a negative sexual experience."

She looked away. "Neither do I, exactly. I don't remember the actual incident. It was weeks later when Sebastian approached me with the video clip."

His voice was low and hurried. "So sex is positive for you?"

She moved away from him. "We need to get back to a more professional rapport. Your questions are rather intrusive and personal."

Alistair reached out and grasped her arm, pulling her back towards him. In a lowered voice, he said, "I'm much more interested in the personal relationship."

Placing her hands on his chest, she said, "It wouldn't serve either of us to rush into something. It's too complicated."

"I'll invest into Gala & More as a silent partner." Moving his hands to her hips, he drew her closer to him.

She looked away from him. "We agreed that Gala & More should organize an event for your company. I want to stick to that agreement."

He stepped back. "I'm willing to re-negotiate that point."

She didn't meet his gaze. "I'm not. I don't want your investment to be tied to whatever happens between us. It's better that we wait."

Anna walked into the mansion and didn't glance

back. She needed a shower. He was so transparent. He was interested in a sexual encounter. But she had no desire to further complicate their relationship. She may not have any negative feelings about her physical safety around men, but she had a hard time trusting them emotionally.

Her father had let her down throughout her entire childhood and then Sebastian made her question her judgment about men. She hadn't told Alistair that she had been dating Sebastian when the incident happened. He dated all the women he had taken advantage of. She had begun to trust him in some small way until she had woken up on the football field, naked without a stitch of clothing in sight. He had wanted to have sex and she said she wasn't ready.

Stepping into her room, she closed the door and tried to wipe the past from her mind. She called Frances and told her about the vineyard.

Running a hot bath, she stripped out of her clothing, and after getting off the phone, she sank into the luxurious tub.

She would have to face Alistair over dinner. Somehow, she needed to figure out how to move their association back to a more professional footing. The desire building between them was not helpful. She needed to figure out how to save Gala & More and not allow herself to be drawn into an affair with him. Nothing good would come of it. Climbing out of the tub after a long soak, she went in search of jeans and a T-shirt.

Realizing she had either work boots or heels, she vowed to pack more options next time. She slipped on the heels and headed downstairs.

Walking down the staircase, she caught sight of Alistair in a pressed formal shirt and dress pants. He looked clean-shaven and polished.

"I thought you insisted on casual dress for dinner."

He smiled at her. "I thought you liked to dress for dinner."

She bit her lip. "Not if I know you'll be dressed casually."

He gestured towards the upstairs. "Do you want to change?"

She shook her head. "No, I'm exhausted and starving."

He led her onto the terrace. She was enjoying her stay at the vineyard. The guesthouse was large and ornate, but it reminded her of a traditional home.

Alistair opened a bottle of cabernet from a special reserve and she asked, "Will I be able to meet your grandparents while I'm here?"

"We can visit them before we leave."

Alistair poured a glass of wine for her and then for himself.

"Staying in this house and being on the vineyard, I'm getting a sense of their life and would like to meet them." She took a sip of wine and wondered why she was so curious about them. Maybe she wanted to see another side of Alistair.

The housekeeper served a salad, then a beef stew, along with fresh baked bread.

She thought about the vineyard and the employees. It reminded her of a large family. They all took great care with the vines and seemed to enjoy being part of the vineyard.

They ate in silence for several minutes until she said, "My muscles are sore, especially my arms. I didn't realize how exhausting it would be."

He took a sip of wine. "You're a surprisingly good worker."

She looked up at him. "I've always enjoyed gardening and working outside."

"How are your hands?" He held out his, palm up.

She turned over her hand and placed it in his for him to inspect.

"Not amazing." Earlier in the bath, she had noticed numerous scrapes and a few blisters forming.

He lightly traced her fingers with his and a heat spread up her arm. She removed her hand and took a sip of wine.

The housekeeper cleared their plates and asked about coffee.

Anna shook her head and then Alistair thanked the woman and wished her goodnight.

Alistair poured them both more wine. "I'll show you the how the grapes are processed tomorrow and then we can have tea with my grandparents at three or four o'clock and head back to London. Do you have an event you need to be back for?"

The night was creating a more intimate atmosphere between them. "There is an event, but Elyse and Katie are handling it."

He leaned back in his chair. "Did today give you any ideas for the launch?"

"I've been thinking a lot about an outside venue for the celebration and I keep coming back to using a public garden."

Alistair watched her with a hooded gaze. He drew

her in easily and she wanted to throw caution to the wind and let herself be seduced by him.

"I agree. An outside venue will add interest."

Standing up, she said, "I have a few emails to send, so I'll say goodnight."

He stood up. "Sleep well."

Walking away from him wasn't easy.

***

Anna woke up early and got dressed in jeans and a T-shirt. Instead of pruning the vines today, she was supposed to spend time with Alistair in the production area. The grapes weren't ready to harvest yet, but the workers were getting the equipment ready and accepting deliveries of the supplies.

The house was quiet, so she ventured outside and took a few photographs. The morning sun coming over the vineyard created a spectacular image of the vines and gently sloping hills. How did Alistair leave this place? If she managed the vineyard, she doubted that she would spend any time in London.

Alistair joined her on the terrace and brought her a cup of coffee. He was wearing worn jeans and a black T-shirt with work boots.

"You're an early riser."

She looked out over the vineyard. "I like to be awake when everything is quiet."

"Is that a habit you started when working for Blackly Simonson?"

She could see a mist rising off the vines as the sun started to warm the earth. Shaking her head, she said, "No. I've always woken up early. My mother used to insist that I needed fewer hours of sleep than most."

Alistair looked at her with an intensity that made her body ache to be touched. "A good trait for a managing partner to have."

The day passed in a blur. She accompanied Alistair on his morning rounds but then ventured out on her own. The crew he had working at the vineyard had been together a long time and everyone was welcoming and ready to show her different aspects of the business.

She was helping to reload labels into a machine when Alistair caught her attention.

"It's nearly three o'clock, and my grandparents are expecting us in the next hour."

She nodded and thanked the worker she was helping. Walking out of the production facility, she waved to different people she had met.

They headed back to the guesthouse to shower. Anna packed her belongings and met Alistair in the foyer. He carried their bags to the car and she reluctantly followed.

He opened the boot of the car. "I could leave you here for a week and you wouldn't notice that I was gone."

She smiled at him. "I'd notice."

He met her gaze. "You definitely made a good impression."

They both climbed into the Land Rover.

Maneuvering down the driveway, he asked, "Did it give you a better idea of what to do for the event?"

Anna glanced out the window. "Yes. But, now I'm obsessed with the idea of living on a vineyard. I don't know how you leave this place."

Slowing down near the main gate, he said, "The

business is much larger than just producing the wine. There is also the sales and distribution network to manage."

She thought about the business aspects of Martin Enterprises. "Everyone I met yesterday and today seemed dedicated and happy. I've observed it at your corporate offices and at the microbreweries. I'm sure very few organizations get to that level of loyalty and clarity."

"It's part of being a strong leader. I actively cultivate an organization that seeks simplicity, continuous improvement, and dedication to the overall mission."

Looking out the window, she realized Alistair was so much more than just a man who inherited a vineyard. He had the intellect and insight to grow the business and ensure its success.

"I know Gala & More is much smaller, but I want to learn to do some of the same things."

"I guess it's advantageous that you have a business advisor."

Something told her that he would be setting out more growth opportunities for her in the near future. She wanted to wrap up his event so she could be free to pursue a physical relationship with him. But would she regret getting involved with him?

***

Alistair turned down the driveway marked "private" on the other side of the vineyard. After a considerable distance, his grandparent's cottage came into view.

"It's beautiful. Is it historic?"

"No. It was built five years ago with the intent to

have old world charm, but it offers all of the modern conveniences."

He parked in the front circle and came around to join her. She had stepped out of the vehicle and was straightening her skirt and running a hand through her hair.

"I hope having guests doesn't put them out."

He placed his hand on her lower back and guided her up the front path. "They're excited to meet you. Don't worry. Life here at the vineyard is more relaxed than London."

He had called to warn them that she was a Bolles. His grandparents were not huge fans of Oliver Bolles. There had been bad blood between Oliver and his father over a series of gambling debts. He had never completely understood all the nuances, but his grandfather blamed Oliver for trying to financially ruin his son.

His relationship with both of his grandparents had become close, but he had never taken an interest in his father's life. The man had chosen not to acknowledge him, and by the time his grandparents had reached out, he was dead. It was almost as if the man didn't exist, except occasionally he would see a sad look on one of his grandparents' faces, and in that moment the grief was palpable.

His grandmother opened the door and invited them in. She was in her gardening clothes, still holding her gloves, and had a scarf on her head.

"I lost track of time. I must apologize. Please come in and I'll go and wash up."

Alistair watched his grandmother disappear. "That was my grandmother, Rose Martin. She'll be back in a few minutes. My grandfather is probably on the back porch."

He brought her through the cottage to an expansive enclosed porch along the back of the house. His grandfather sat in his favorite chair, reading the newspaper.

"Granddad, I'd like you to meet Anna Bolles."

His grandfather stood up and folded his paper. "It's nice to meet you Ms. Bolles. Please call me Arthur."

She shook his hand and said, "Anna, please."

His grandfather gestured to the sofa and Anna sat down. Alistair had never brought a woman over to formally meet his grandparents. They had met some of his dates out at events, but he had never brought a woman over to meet them.

"I don't know where Rose is. Maybe the garden?" His granddad relied on his wife to make small talk.

Alistair sat next to Anna. "She let us in and is washing up. We've spent a couple of days at the vineyard."

His grandfather sat down. "The harvest isn't long off. We'll see how some of your new varieties work out."

For several minutes, they discussed the weather and how it would affect the harvest.

His grandmother came in carrying a tray with tea and biscuits.

Everyone stood up. Alistair said, "Nan, this is Anna Bolles. My grandmother, Rose Martin."

Anna smiled and said, "It's lovely to meet you, Mrs. Martin."

"You as well, my dear. Please call me Rose."

Rose placed a three-tier cake stand at the center of the table with a layer of sandwiches, a layer of cakes, and a layer of scones. She then set out plates and teacups.

"Anna, would you like Earl Grey, peppermint, chamomile, green tea?" Rose asked.

"Peppermint, please." Anna accepted the teacup.

His grandmother served him and his grandfather Earl Grey and then peppermint for herself.

He served his grandfather and then Anna a small sandwich and a scone. He waited a moment for his grandmother.

Rose said, "I'm fine with tea, dear."

"Everything looks delicious," Anna said and took a small bite.

Alistair sat next to Anna and waited for the questions to begin.

"I knew your father," Rose offered.

Anna placed her teacup down. "Unfortunately, I didn't know him well. I saw him occasionally when I was a young child, and then years went by, and then I saw him shortly before he died."

"I'm sorry. You must have been very young when he passed." His grandmother didn't believe in ignoring basic truths.

Anna glanced down at her hands. "Seventeen."

She had been young. Alistair thought Oliver had been more involved in her life, but he was often in New York with his other family. In some ways, they had a similar experience. He grew up without his father and often wondered what he was like and why he had made the choices he had. His father wasn't nearly as wealthy or well known as Oliver Bolles.

Oliver had made a fortune in investment banking, while his father gambled away the assets of the vineyard. It wasn't until the last ten years or so that the family regained and expanded their wealth.

Anna turned to Rose. "I loved the vineyard. Everything about it. The vines go on for miles and miles and then the people that have been with the vineyard forever were so friendly and helpful."

His grandmother smiled at Anna. "Alistair tells us that you are going to help put together a launch party for a new wine and a harvest celebration."

"We're considering one of the public gardens on the outskirts of London. It'll give the garden a boost in funding and then also provide a beautiful outside venue."

Rose looked at her husband and smiled before turning to Anna. "It sounds marvelous."

His grandparents had been slightly put off when he mentioned bringing Anna over, but they seemed relaxed and at ease.

His grandmother smiled at Anna. "Would you like to see my garden?"

Anna stood. "I'd love to."

He watched the two of them walk out arm in arm.

His grandfather said, "You've made Nan happy. I bet she will talk of little else in the coming week."

He stood and served himself another sandwich. "I met her years ago. Her sister is married to Fionn Lynch."

"Are you involved with her?" his granddad asked.

Alistair sat down and placed his plate on the table. "Not exactly. We have a business relationship at the moment and she is holding me to that, but after the event I plan on pursuing something more."

His granddad hesitated and then said, "Don't trivialize the Bolles legacy. Her father was not a good man."

Alistair ran a hand through his hair. "She wasn't raised by Oliver."

"They say she has his mathematical ability. She probably has his logical thinking and ability with cards."

Alistair laughed. "Do you know how absurd that sounds? My father and Oliver were from a different generation and did get involved with gambling. I've never had the urge to gamble, and from what I can tell neither does Anna."

His grandfather frowned. "I hope she's nothing like him."

"Yes, but you have to admit that we are seeing things from the Martin side, and maybe not with enough perspective. I'm sure Oliver Bolles had his reasons."

His grandfather had a distant look and Alistair lapsed into silence. He shouldn't have pushed him. Granddad wanted to remember the good things about his son, not the problems.

His grandmother and Anna returned from the garden, chatting and laughing.

He met Anna's gaze. "I'm sorry, but we need to head back."

Rose touched his arm. "Are you sure you can't stay for supper?"

He looked at his grandmother's hopeful face. "I'll invite Anna again, but I need to be in London this evening."

They said a hurried goodbye and left the cottage. It had been a mistake bringing her to meet them. He didn't want to disappoint either one of his grandparents. He preferred to keep his personal life to himself. They were desperate for him to settle down, and while his grandfather held a grudge against Oliver Bolles, his grandmother seemed ready to embrace Anna. But he wasn't sure that he wanted a serious relationship. What if she wanted something from him that he wasn't capable of giving? Fionn was right about him. He wasn't a safe bet. He would rather be alone in the world then trapped into a meaningless existence.

Chapter 6

The following week, Anna received a text from Alistair cancelling their standing appointment on Wednesday. He had been distant since visiting the vineyard.

He was staying in Costa Rica for a few more days, but when he returned on the weekend, he asked to attend an event she was coordinating. She responded with the information on the launch for a new cosmetics line on Saturday evening.

Anna added him to an invite list and continued to work on the event. In between, she managed to visit three public gardens and stopped in to see Frances and the baby. She held the little girl while Frances put on tea and helped her brainstorm ideas for Alistair's event.

"The biggest issue you are going to have, besides the lack of a real kitchen, is the terrain. Women will wear heels, so you'll have to find a cost effective way to put down some type of material to create a walking path."

Anna nodded, relishing the sensation of the warm bundle in her arms. She had enjoyed her nieces as infants, but something had shifted in her recently, and she had begun to crave a baby of her own. It was a crazy idea. She needed to focus on the business.

Frances poured tea for them. "I'm sorry to abandon you right now. It's just my mother was always working and I want to be home with her. You understand, right?"

Anna placed the baby in the nearby bassinet. "Yes. You are being immensely helpful by weighing in and helping me brainstorm."

Finishing her tea, she hugged Frances. She didn't even allow herself to glance at the baby. She didn't want to long for something that was impossible at the moment.

She took a taxi to Olivia's studio after leaving Frances. She wanted to see her nieces.

Ringing the bell, an assistant opened the door and invited her in. Her nieces were drawing and using glitter at a small table set in the back of the studio. The oldest, Beatrice, jumped up when she saw Anna.

Making eye contact with Olivia, she asked "Could I take the girls to the park for an hour?"

Olivia put down the fabric she was holding and said, "It'll be an unexpected treat for them. It'll give their nanny a chance to go home and prepare their tea. Just drop them off at home?"

Her nieces were dressed in their play clothes. The five-year-old, Beatrice, kept up a conversation throughout the six-block walk while Anna chased after the two-year-old, Addy, getting her to drop things she picked up from the sidewalk.

She took a few brief phone calls while she watched the two play in the park. The day was warm for September and when Addy insisted on being carried, Anna called out to Beatrice, knowing it was time to go.

Walking back to their house with Addy in her arms, she relaxed. Her nieces were full of love and happiness. She kissed them both goodbye on the doorstep, and when the nanny took them inside, she waved and walked back down the path to the street.

***

The night of the cosmetics launch, Anna found it difficult to focus. The addition of a dozen or so models added a heightened tension. There were complaints about the lighting and the product samples were late. Katie had opened the shipment that morning and had discovered the wrong order had been sent, so she had to drive two hours each way to pick up the right product.

When Anna arrived at the venue, hundreds of gift bags needed to be assembled.

The product manager for the launch, Judy, glared at her. "Why didn't you check the order before this morning?"

The woman was relentless. In a calm, controlled voice, Anna said, "I apologize for the oversight. My staff will make it work."

Judy stamped her heel on the floor and clenched her hands into fists. "I need this evening to be flawless."

Noticing a ladder was not properly secured, Anna said, "It will be. Please excuse me." The maintenance staff was changing out light bulbs and Anna rushed over to alert them.

She motioned for the foreman to deal with it. She called the caterer to remind them about having a nut-free table for hors d'oeuvres.

The florist brought in large displays of flowers and Judy began complaining about the overpowering fragrance.

If the woman yelled her name one more time across the ballroom, Anna was not going to be responsible for her actions. Why would Gala & More have taken on this event?

Elyse arrived at that moment and distracted her. The maintenance staff finished the lighting change and retreated from the ballroom. Elyse helped her position the tables and Anna thought the set-up looked amazing.

Anna spoke with the florist about the fragrance and they let her know Judy had changed the order a few days ago. Anna asked them to remove the displays and come up with another solution. She needed flowers with almost no fragrance. Why would Judy mess with the order?

Katie and Elyse were filling the giveaway cosmetics bags. Anna hoped it would come together. Everyone who was part of this event was on edge. There were so many undercurrents, Anna couldn't tell where her time should be spent.

Somehow, all the pieces came together and they were able to open the doors on time.

The models took turns handing out the gift bags and talking up the new line of cosmetics. The event was well attended. After it was underway, she didn't speak with Judy again. She hoped to avoid the woman for the remainder of the evening.

Anna was in the kitchen when she noticed Alistair arrive on the monitor. She studied his reaction to the event for a moment and then she watched a model approach him. The tall, slim, red-haired model offered him a sample bag, but he declined. The model seemed to hang on his every word. Anna could feel her irritation building. She reminded herself Alistair was a business associate. It wouldn't help anything to become jealous.

She gave a few instructions to the caterer, then headed out into the event to greet Alistair.

He caught her gaze and retreated from the model.

"I was beginning to think you weren't onsite." His tone was sharp.

She gaze swept over the room. "I wish I wasn't onsite and I didn't want to interrupt your conversation."

He checked his watch. "Show me the event—and I'd like to meet the client."

Her stomach plummeted. Judy would invariably complain about every detail. She hadn't had one pleasant thing to say all day.

She turned away from the guests and said quietly, "Alistair, they demanded a run of the mill event. No surprises. Nothing special—and then tried to make last minute adjustments themselves. The client is impossible and I'd rather not introduce you."

He paused before saying, "Knowing how to manage difficult clients is part of the business."

Moving closer to him, she lowered her voice further. "Can you evaluate another event?"

Placing his hands in his pockets, he said, "I've a packed schedule and we agreed on this event."

Anna looked around the ballroom and turned back to Alistair. She gripped his arm. "Please. Make an exception. Trust me on this. It won't be pleasant."

Judy walked over and interrupted them. "Is there an issue, Ms. Bolles?"

Anna let go of his arm. "No, not at all." After a brief moment, she said, "I'd like to introduce Alistair Martin to you."

Before she completed the introduction, Judy gushed, "I've heard so much about you, Mr. Martin. The pleasure is all mine."

Anna walked away from them. She didn't want to hear the bitter woman's interpretation of the event. She had worked incredibly hard and was ready to move on.

Guests were beginning to leave so she reminded those working the event to stay attentive and to keep the tables cleared.

It was nine o'clock by the time she was ready to leave the hotel. Alistair had messaged her to say he was waiting at the hotel bar.

She didn't want to face Alistair's critique of her work. She had missed him and didn't look forward to discussing the company tonight. Walking into the bar, she caught sight of him having a pint and watching a football match.

Anna slid onto the stool next to him. The bartender put a napkin down in front of her and she asked for a Guinness.

"Were you happy with the event?"

Anna could feel her anxiety rise. It wasn't a stellar effort by Gala & More, but the client was exceedingly difficult. "There were some adjustments that had to be dealt with at the last moment. I agree that there could have been better planning."

He took a swallow of his ale. "What would you have changed?"

"The flower arrangements were too high and the pervasive lily scent messed with the perfume scent in the launch. The lighting hadn't been changed the day before so it caused craziness during the set-up. The samples shipped to Gala & More were incorrect so Katie had to drive four hours to get the right samples. I could go on."

He met her gaze. "I'm getting the sense you aren't particularly concerned."

She shrugged. "I'm not. I've no intention of ever working for that client again. Most if not all of the issues were caused by their mismanagement and lack of communication."

He took another swallow of his ale. "Clients talk, so even if you intend to decline their next event, the negative public relations could hurt Gala & More."

Anna smoothed her dress. "The event, while a struggle, came off well."

Alistair shook his head. "The client isn't satisfied."

Anna crossed her arms. "It would be impossible to make her happy."

He met her gaze and she felt her skin warm. "Have you considered your part in this debacle?"

Looking away, she said, "My part? I worked extremely hard on this event."

His voice was controlled and low. "Yes, but why didn't your hard work pay off?"

Anna thought about her role in the event. They were understaffed for the number of events that they had taken on. "I should have been double-checking the details, knowing that the client withheld information and had high impossible standards."

Alistair ran a hand through his hair. "True. But you also need to assert your authority. Call the client if they communicate directly with the florist and tell them that behavior is unacceptable. Insist that all your vendors check with you on any changes."

She thought about the line between taking over and being flexible. "The client has the ultimate say on the elements of the event."

Alistair touched her knee and a slow warmth spread up her legs.

"I don't agree. The event becomes a reflection on Gala & More. You need to protect your reputation."

Trying to ignore his hand, she said, "I can't force my vision on them."

He removed his hand and took out his wallet. "You need to let the client know that once they sign the contract and agree on the overall concept and budget that they need to leave the details to you. A small decision about changing the flower arrangements could ruin an event and probably did."

Anna wanted to go home and lick her wounds in private. "Point taken."

Taking a last swallow of his ale, he put a few pounds on the counter. "I'd like to visit the venue you are recommending for my event tonight."

Anna slid off her stool. "As long as you keep in mind once we agree on the concept, you will need to leave the details to me."

He laughed. "I'm not just a client. Am I?"

They walked out of the hotel and Alistair gave his ticket to the valet. She had let Katie take the hired car home an hour ago and was going to get a taxi.

Alistair drove through London and she checked

her messages. She had a fundraising event tomorrow.

She said, "There won't be lights on tonight. But I have a key." She looked through her bag and found the small, white envelope with the key.

"They gave you a key."

He was gorgeous. Everything about him drew her interest. His voice, his mannerisms, the way he held his athletic body and the intensity of his gaze. "I presented the concept at their committee meeting and they're excited."

He asked about her week and she gave him a rundown on all the complexities she had faced.

Alistair pulled into the secluded parking area. It was a darker night than when she had visited a week ago.

Anna used the antique key in the garden gate to unlock it and then slipped it into her bag.

Her eyes adjusted within a minute or two, but she stumbled on the rocky path. Alistair reached out and steadied her. "This terrain is going to be a problem."

"There will be outside lighting and I've researched a few products that could be used to provide temporary walkways."

She loved this garden. Her grandmother had taken her several times as a young girl. It had been in existence for two hundred years. There were small gathering spaces and wide-open lawns to host events. She was thinking of using an old stone foundation on the property. Anna led Alistair to the left and down a moss-covered path.

The foundation was about three hundred feet from the gate, and at one time a barn was erected on the site. The area within the foundation was level and could accommodate tables for two hundred people.

Anna gestured to the foundation. "This is a unique space that I think could remind wine connoisseurs of the feeling of going into a wine cellar."

Alistair looked over the space. "It's going to take a huge amount of effort and money to transform this."

Trying to slow down her rate of speech, she said, "The investment is substantial, but you would have the added benefit of supporting a public garden."

He watched her closely. "Do the dates work? What about the caterer?"

She nodded. "The date is set aside for you. I'm in the process of interviewing caterers that specialize in outside dining."

"Gala & More will need to put together a comprehensive budget. The ground covering, rentals, lighting."

"I've been working on it and should have it together by Wednesday."

He turned to look at her. "This is a magnificent venue."

She could barely see his facial expressions, but his tone was positive. Relief flooded through her body. He liked the concept.

"You have hidden talents, Ms. Bolles."

Anna moved forward to see his expression. It was impossible to get a read on him.

He lightly touched her arm and pulled her closer. She reached out to steady herself and could feel warmth emanating from his chest.

He was within inches of her and said, "I love your fragrance."

Capturing her head with his hands, he lowered his mouth and kissed her lightly before pulling back. Waiting for him to kiss her properly, she drew in a breath. He traced her lips with his tongue, before fully exploring her mouth.

She returned his kisses, clinging to him. His breath sounded harsh when he finally pulled back and said, "I can't get enough of you."

The darkness surrounded them and she moved forward and kissed his neck. He turned her and captured her mouth again. She tugged on his shirt and lifted it from his pants. He let out a groan when she ran her hands over his warm, sculpted chest. He pulled up her dress and ran his hands over her bottom, pulling her closer.

Anna could feel desire course through her body and moved closer to feel his chest. She wanted more of him. She wanted to move against his erection, but held back.

"Anna, I want to take you home tonight." He touched her breast and she couldn't think.

She leaned her head against his chest and could feel his heartbeat. "We have to wait until the business aspect of our relationship is settled."

"You want a promise of an investment before you have sex with me?" He ran his hands over her back. "Fine. I'll invest."

She attempted to move away from him, but he held her tightly. "No. I want to move forward in a relationship with you regardless of whether you invest or not. It just can't affect the outcome. It would be unfair to the others involved in the company."

"I don't get it." He continued to caress her bottom

and drew her closer to his erection.

She pushed away slightly. "The investment shouldn't rely on our relationship. It should stand on its own merit. I need to complete the event and then you can decide to invest or to walk away."

He let go of her and her dress fell back into place. "You're willing to put aside your desire for weeks?"

Stepping away from him, she said, "It's the right thing to do, Alistair."

Alistair tucked his shirt back in. "I don't necessarily agree but I get it."

Anna retraced her steps to the Land Rover. She needed to move forward with her ideas and stop obsessing about her craving for him. Would they be able to wait? Or would she cave in to her desire? It seemed unfair that she had known him for so long but now needed to wait for the business transaction to be concluded. It's not what she wanted, but it was the right thing to do.

Chapter 7

Anna woke early with a nervous feeling in her stomach. She and Elyse were set to drive down that morning to present the final details to Martin Enterprises.

Over the last two weeks, she barely had contact with Alistair, and instead had been working on events Gala & More had already been contracted to manage. The wine launch would be the first event that she had conceived of and designed herself. She had driven Frances and Elyse insane with the details, but she was ready.

Alistair had told her in a conference call that he was going to assemble his sales and marketing teams to give their stamp of approval. There would be at least six people attending the meeting.

She met Elyse at the office and the assembled the needed samples and materials for the presentation.

Getting into the small hired car, Anna said, "I hope this goes well. So much is riding on putting together a brilliant event."

Elyse said, "You've done a wonderful job. Each time I've heard the presentation, I was sold. Remember, positive thoughts."

During the drive, they discussed other projects

and reminded each other to relax.

They parked behind the building, allowing them to carry in the samples and materials. Anna had emailed the presentation the day before so Alistair's assistant could set up the conference room. Katie had bound and copied a dozen color proposals to hand out.

In the parking area, Elyse reached out and touched her elbow. "You've got this. Your presentation is engaging and you've thought of everything."

Anna hugged her. "I appreciate all of your help." In the last few weeks, she had become close to Elyse and Katie. The company was beginning to come together.

She opened the boot and took out the cart they had purchased for events. Elyse helped her load all the boxes and materials.

Anna was familiar with Martin Enterprises and led Elyse to the conference room, after saying hello to the receptionist.

Alistair's assistant, Ryan, was getting the room ready and helped them unpack the boxes. Anna advanced the first digital slide and thanked Ryan for uploading it. Elyse placed the proposals in front of the chairs for each person that would be seated at the table.

The other samples and materials were set up on a side table and included a place setting, linens, flowers, lights and the fabric that would cover the pathway.

Pacing in front of the podium, Anna took a deep breath and waited for the attendees to come in. Mentally reviewing the concept in her head, she reminded herself to slow down and remember to get a read on her audience. Elyse stood off to the side and would help answer questions and distribute samples.

Alistair was the first to arrive and greeted both her and Elyse before speaking with Ryan.

The sales and marketing executives came in and Alistair introduced everyone before taking a seat at the end of the long table.

Anna tried not to focus on Alistair, but her gaze kept returning to him. Since their passionate encounter at the public garden, the tension between them was palpable. Each time she thought about becoming romantically involved with him, she reconsidered her position, but came back to the same issue. For his part, Alistair hadn't brought it up or made any attempt to change her mind. She was certain if he had she would crumble. These days, her desire for him occupied most of her thoughts.

Alistair nodded, and she addressed the executives. She began her pitch with a brief background of Gala & More. The team assembled seemed receptive and friendly.

She explained the concept for the evening and clicked through images of the venue. She stepped back when she launched a short animation of the nighttime dinner with the tables, linens, and chairs in place. She stopped it twice to point out particular features. Keeping an eye on her audience, she noticed they seemed engaged.

Elyse turned the lights back on and Anna gestured towards the proposals that had been placed in front of them. She went through the costs and all of the elements she had considered. Elyse passed around samples of the ground covering and pointed to the samples for the linens and place settings.

She opened up the presentation to questions and noted that most of the concerns raised were around the flow of the event and making sure the sales team would be able to talk about the wine.

Alistair said, "Thank you. If you want to wait in reception with Ryan, we'll talk through your proposal and will let you know if the concept works for us."

Ryan served them coffee in the upstairs reception area. She and Elyse spoke about another event and tried not to obsess about the deliberations.

After twenty minutes, Alistair called them back into the conference room and indicated that they should sit. The podium had been moved and the smart board was turned off. Anna began to have a sinking feeling. Alistair had been committed to mentoring her, but maybe his team had another idea they favored.

"I explained to my team that if Gala & More was selected by Martin Enterprises that it was more than a commitment to an event. We would be bringing on your company for all event management over the next year and I was considering an investment into Gala & More."

Anna met his gaze. He was deciding early. He wasn't going to wait until the event unfolded.

He smiled at her. "Your concept for the celebration won everyone over. We've selected Gala & More to manage the event and become our preferred events management company."

Shock sifted over her. She had worked so hard on the concept, but she hadn't let herself believe that they would use her concept.

Anna stood up, saying, "I greatly appreciate your

vote of confidence in Gala & More." She smiled at Elyse and looked back at the executives around the table. "We can't wait to start."

After a few more questions, Elyse and Anna began to pack up the materials and samples. Everyone on staff was positive and congratulatory.

Alistair walked them out and asked for a moment with Anna.

Stepping away from the car, Alistair said, "My team was impressed. Instead of adding another layer of pressure to the event, we decided collectively to offer Gala & More the contract for all event planning for the year. I'll reach out to my solicitor to sort out the investment contract."

"Thank you, Alistair."

He held her gaze. "There will be a few stipulations to the agreement, moving to a more appropriate business location and hiring a chartered accountant."

Anna nodded. "It's been part of our long-term plan. But we haven't had the funds."

He smiled. "Let's meet on Monday to sign the contracts and then I'll take you to a celebratory dinner."

She nodded and stepped closer to embrace him. It didn't feel real. Had she really secured a future for Gala & More? What did this mean for them personally? Was he interested in having a fling or something more?

His seductive scent was full of complex spices and his pressed shirt was cool beneath her hands. Stepping back, she caught a look of desire that flashed across his face, but he let her go. She wanted to press her mouth to his, but Elyse was a short distance away loading the car.

She met his gaze. "I can't quite believe we're moving forward."

He kissed her cheek. "Your presentation was flawless." Alistair smiled widely. "Monday cannot come soon enough."

Anna walked back to Elyse and helped her position the last box.

When they were on their way, she said to her, "It's odd. I don't feel anything. I should be over the moon."

"You must be in shock, but the joy will come. Do you want me to drive?"

She focused on driving. "I'm fine. I need something to do. I feel like adrenaline is buzzing through my body."

Elyse called Frances and put her on speaker. They spent the next thirty minutes discussing the investment and how to move forward.

After dropping Elyse off at her flat, Anna gave her mother a call. The housekeeper told her that her mother had gone on a three-week cruise and was expected back in four days. She decided not to call Olivia. She wasn't ready to discuss her relationship with Alistair. She wasn't even sure if it was a relationship.

Anna was at loose ends. She had worked hard to earn the investment, but now she felt unsettled instead of happy. Deciding to go for a run, she went back to her dingy flat and changed. The entire run was spent thinking about Alistair. Her feelings for him were intensifying. Why didn't he wait until after the event to announce the investment? Had he decided to rush things so they could pursue a physical relationship?

***

By the following Monday, Anna accepted that Alistair had changed the rules. His solicitor had reached out to her and she had put them in touch with the solicitor that Olivia had recommended. Her solicitor had reviewed the contract and drew up a partnership agreement with Frances that included buyout clauses in case one of them wanted to leave the company.

Anna took Monday off to get a haircut, facial, and stop by to see Olivia. She decided on a short, stylish dress and four-inch heels.

Arriving at the solicitor's office a few minutes early, she was welcomed and brought into a conference room. Her solicitor arrived with the documents already signed by Frances and the meeting took place. She was disappointed that Alistair didn't come; he had signed the documents and sent a check via courier.

"Congratulations, Ms. Bolles. I wish you the best of luck with your endeavor."

Anna handed all of the documentation to her solicitor along with the check to hold for two days, giving each party in the transaction the right to cancel the investment in the next forty-eight hours. He shook her hand and headed back to his offices.

Deciding to walk a few blocks to a local park, Anna caught sight of Alistair leaning against a Trident Iceni, his low-slung sports car in metallic gray. He was wearing sunglasses, obscuring his eyes, but smiled broadly at her.

Anna hesitated briefly before walking to him.

"Your legs are gorgeous in that dress."

"That's what you're choosing to say to me?"

He took his glasses off and stepped closer to her. "We're on a busy street, love."

She tried to keep her voice neutral. "You've directed every comment to your solicitor and then you don't even show up for the contract signing."

Alistair opened the door for her. "Let's talk in private."

Anna contemplated walking away, but she wanted to know what he was thinking.

"Anna, please."

She moved past him and climbed into the low car with as much dignity as she could muster.

Alistair closed her door and then went around and got into the driver's seat. He started the powerful engine.

"What happened to your Land Rover?"

"It's a business vehicle. This car is pure pleasure."

They rode in silence for several minutes as Alistair navigated the insane traffic.

She bit down on her lower lip before saying, "Why didn't you come to the meeting?"

Alistair spoke in a flat voice. "It was better to leave it a purely business transaction. As you said, our desire for each other shouldn't influence the deal."

Turning towards him, she said, "You can't be part of a business conversation with me?"

Meeting her gaze briefly, he said, "I'm no longer interested in merely a business association with you."

"Then why did you invest?" Anna watched him

shift gears; they were heading out of the city.

"I knew from the beginning I would invest in Gala & More. With minor tweaking, your company will do well."

She shook her head. "It felt odd for you to be so disconnected from the transaction."

He shifted again and passed another car. "I want us to move past the business aspects. Now that the deal is complete, I intend to focus on the more personal aspects of our relationship."

Anna readjusted her seatbelt. "If you were interested in a personal relationship, then why haven't you called or texted?"

He kept his eyes on the road. "I wanted to give you the space to make a decision not based on longing or desire, but business. Was this the right deal for Gala? Were the terms acceptable?"

She snapped, "It's not that easy. You're completely intertwined in the business decision. You were giving advice and expecting me to jump through hoops for you."

Alistair shrugged. "The night we went to see the public park, you said you needed space to figure out the business issues before anything happened between us."

Anna rubbed her temples. He was impossible to figure out. "Alistair, I felt abandoned by you. Over the last six weeks, I spoke with you daily or communicated through email or texting. But since you decided to invest, your interest has disappeared."

He glanced at her. "I don't know why this is an issue for you. You could have easily picked up the phone or dropped by to see me."

Anna shook her head but said nothing. She didn't feel comfortable reaching out to him. It was true—she had wanted to resolve the business entanglements before she was open to having a relationship, but she wanted his involvement.

Without thinking, she said, "What kind of relationship are you interested in?"

***

Alistair loosened his tight grip on the steering wheel. The question was loaded. "Why don't we take it slowly and see where it leads?"

He didn't understand her. He thought giving her closure on the business and investment would allow them to establish a connection beyond Gala & More. But, she had clearly felt neglected in some way. He wasn't amazing at offering reassurances in a relationship. He knew this about himself. Invariably, he would begin to feel trapped by expectations and move to end the relationship.

He needed the freedom to make decisions about his life without someone else trying to control his every move. Even the expectations of his grandparents and the winery became too much at times. His release was extreme sports. In the last couple of years, even that was becoming less and less effective.

He pulled into his driveway and parked the car, shutting off the engine.

"I'm wildly attracted to you, Anna." He met her gaze. "But I also crave freedom. A trigger for me is feeling trapped by other people's expectations. I'm bringing this up because you seem to need some type of reassurance from me. We're not a good match in that way."

Anna blinked a few times. "I get it. I value my independence as well. I'm not looking for a permanent commitment, but I'm curious where you see this heading."

He'd upset her. He could see it in her downcast gaze and the tension in her body.

He turned more fully towards her. "Maybe you're not looking for marriage right now, but there is something that upsets you about not being certain of an emotional attachment."

"I'm not interested in a one-night adventure."

He reached forward and kissed her fleetingly. "I organized a celebratory dinner. Let's enjoy the evening and then I'll take you home when you are ready."

Instead of waiting for her to object, he bolted out of the car, walked around and opened her door.

He offered her his hand and gently tugged her from the low vehicle. Her legs looked amazing in her patterned stockings and wickedly high heels. He could feel the blood rushing to his male anatomy and made a point of imagining his housekeeper serving dinner. He needed to be patient and not rush her.

She smoothed down the bottom of her short dress. "The house looks quiet without two hundred guests milling about."

He placed his arm around her and they walked up the front path. "The final count was almost three hundred, but it raised the needed funding."

She visibly relaxed when he moved the discussion away from their personal relationship.

Opening the front door, he asked, "Are you wearing another Olivia Bolles creation?"

Anna smiled. "Yes. This is coming out in her spring collection."

He watched her walk into the house. "Your sister has enormous talent."

Stepping away from him, she said, "Do you ever get lost in this mansion?"

He could see she wanted to keep the conversation away from their attraction to each other. "It's large for one person. Even with a housekeeper and gardener. It came on the market and the location and architecture appealed to me. I planned to entertain and assumed one day that I would have a family."

***

Anna moved into the formal living room. It was light out and she could see the English garden in the back.

Alistair didn't shy away from emotions. He told her he craved his freedom and knew that she had abandonment issues. She did. Her father was terrible to her and her mother wasn't much better. Besides having Olivia and William in her life, she had developed very few emotional ties since her grandmother had died five years ago. She had been very busy over the last few years, but her aunt and uncle had reached out to her on numerous occasions. Maybe she shouldn't resist their attempts to draw her closer. She didn't want to live her life not trusting others.

He drew her from her thoughts. "Some champagne to celebrate our deal."

Anna took the glass he offered, and raising it, she said, "To our business deal."

He smiled and touched her glass with his.

She took a swallow. "It is one of your sparkling wines?"

"No. I prefer mine, but it's good to branch out occasionally."

He led her to an elaborately set dining room. His housekeeper served them a salad with roasted walnuts and goat cheese, followed by salmon with a lemon mint dressing.

Throughout the meal, Alistair offered stories about learning the wine business in his early twenties. His grandparents were at his side, but they also had a dedicated and loyal staff.

"Did you grow up knowing who your father was?" Anna asked him.

"No. My mother had decided to sever all ties. He wasn't supportive of the pregnancy and she was afraid he would reject me."

She thought about Alistair as a young boy growing up without a father. "How did you meet your grandparents?"

He hesitated, then said, "When I was fifteen, my mother received a letter from my grandparents telling her that my father had been killed in a car crash. She decided to allow them to see me, and three days later they were on our doorstep. It took nearly a week, but they convinced her to leave her life behind and come to the U.K."

Anna took a sip of champagne. "Does your mother live near here?"

Taking a bite of salmon, Alistair shook his head. "She married two years ago and has settled back in Ireland."

She thought about some of the stories that Fionn

had shared about their early life in Ireland together. Their mothers had been friends and Fionn had tried to protect him. Alistair was five years younger and didn't have anyone looking out for him. "Do you have fond memories about growing up in Ireland?"

Alistair kept his voice neutral. "I don't miss the poverty or my mother having to work all of the time. But I had a tremendous amount of freedom and could get by in school with very little effort."

Anna began to see a different side of the polished and charming man sitting in front of her. He'd had more challenges in his early years that most children. Maybe that was why he was so resilient and determined to make something of himself. "Would you say you are more Irish or English?"

His relaxed voice soothed her nerves. "Both cultures are closely intertwined so I'm not sure. I'm at home in both places."

The sun was setting outside and a warm, dispersed light infiltrated the formal garden. She hoped that their desire for each other was enough. She craved him for so long, she allowed herself to be open to the idea of getting involved. Despite what she said to him in the car, she put the future out of her mind and thought only about tonight.

"Could you show me the garden before it gets dark?"

"Maybe you'll be a gardener in your next career," he said as his gaze flowed over her.

She smiled. "I love to work with plants, but a career is something entirely different."

He took another swallow of champagne. "You'd need a different flat."

She nodded. Her current flat had one window overlooking a brick wall less than two feet away. It definitely didn't work for growing anything.

Alistair stood up and placed his cloth napkin on the table. He opened the door to the terrace and led her into the night air. It reminded her of their first kiss in Olivia's backyard years ago. And their last kiss had been in the public garden. Maybe she was tempting fate by asking him to show her the garden.

He activated the lights from the terrace and led her through the formal spaces. "You probably know much more than I do about the plantings and types of trees."

She explored the grounds. "I grew up with an elaborate garden. My grandmother would come and stay with us sometimes. She spent a ton of time planting and weeding. I learned a great deal from her."

He reached out and took her hand. "Are you suitably impressed?"

Anna had a difficult time concentrating on the garden with her hand held in his. "It's beautiful. There are many old trees and plantings which can't be reproduced."

Pulling her closer to him, he looked into her eyes, and his desire was unmistakable. "I had the gardener plant a fig tree over here in honor of our first kiss."

Her heart fluttered in her chest. She couldn't believe that he had held onto the sentimental memory. "He must have thought it was a bad idea."

She turned and searched the area for the fig tree.

Alistair laughed softly. "Fig trees aren't typical in English gardens, but he humored me."

Anna moved forward and touched the tree. It had

been there for a long time. "When did you have it planted?"

He came up behind her and touched her waist. "The spring after Fionn and Olivia's wedding."

She gasped and covered her mouth. "It doesn't seem like something you would do."

Pulling her back against his chest, he said in a low voice, "I had just purchased the house. It surprised me, but I felt driven to do it. I definitely enjoy the memory."

She allowed herself to remember that night. He fascinated her and she had acted on impulse. "You weren't pleased to discover who I was."

He kissed her neck. "If I recall correctly, you approached me. But only after I had spent the evening slowly encouraging your interest."

Turning she glanced up at him. "I thought you hadn't noticed me until I practically threw myself at you."

"I watched you walk down the aisle during the wedding and something inside of me changed. I can't explain it."

Alistair stood under the tree and waited. She moved closer to him and touched his chest. Standing up on her toes, she gently pressed her lips to his. He moved and pulled her closer, deepening the kiss.

She could feel his entire body pressed close to her, but focused on meeting the demands of his mouth. After a few minutes, he had to pull away briefly to take in oxygen.

"I've waited forever for you," he murmured, his voice husky.

He plundered her mouth again and gently pulled

up her dress, exploring her round, firm bottom. She could feel desire build within her core and wanted him to touch her everywhere.

Alistair pressed his lips to her neck. "You're so beautiful, Anna."

She ran her hands over his chest and began to unbutton his shirt. He returned to her mouth and kissed her again. She continued to unbutton his shirt, and after several clumsy attempts, he stilled her hands and unbuttoned his shirt himself.

She explored his warm chest and ran her hands along his tight muscles.

He stopped kissing her and asked, "Are you sure, Anna? I don't know where this will take us."

Her eyes locked on his, her heart beating fast, and she whispered, "I'm sure."

He led her back through the garden and into the house. The house seemed so much brighter than the garden, and she looked at his bare chest. She stopped herself from placing kisses on his exposed skin and waited for him to do something.

Picking her up, he carried her up the stairs. Anna placed tiny kisses along his jawline.

Taking her into his bedroom, he placed her on the bed. He hastily removed her shoes and followed her silk stockings up to her garter belt. "Your sexy stockings have been driving me crazy all night."

She could hardly believe that they were acting out their desire. "Olivia recommended them. I was wearing gray pants."

He moved onto the bed. "I find you incredibly sexy in anything that you wear."

Anna pushed his shirt off his shoulders. His chest

was defined and tight. She had seen him without a shirt at the beach once, but had kept her distance.

Alistair unrolled her stockings and placed a kiss on the inside of each thigh. He pushed her dress up and kissed her belly.

"I need help with the dress."

She sat up and he slid the zipper down, and then she stood, allowing the dress to fall to the floor.

Alistair stood up and unzipped his dress pants, sliding them down after he kicked off his shoes and removed his socks, balancing on one foot at a time.

He stood in front of her wearing tight black boxers and nothing else.

She released her hair and let it fall down her back. Reaching behind her, she unclasped her bra, and he stepped forward and caught it in his hands.

Removing it completely, he bent down and drew her nipple into his mouth, and she held onto his head. He moved her back against the bed and gently let her fall backwards, his arms around her waist. He followed her and continued exploring her breasts. She was already lost to the sensation and moved against him, wanting more.

"We shouldn't rush this, love."

He moved his hands down her body and tugged off her lace panties. Anna was beyond rational thought. Her entire body was sensitized to his touch and she wanted to feel him against her. She had waited forever for this moment and didn't want to overthink it.

She traced the length of his erection through his boxers and heard his indrawn breath. He put his hand on hers and encouraged her to grip him more firmly.

He stopped kissing her and removed his boxers before looking in his nightstand for a condom.

He put the condom on the bed and captured her wrists, placing them over her head. "You are driving me insane, Anna."

He continued to explore her body and only when she begged him did he rip open the condom and put it on.

Alistair kissed her mouth again and positioned himself over her. She could feel him at her entrance and moved against him. She wanted him inside her.

He steadied her hips, then plunged into her in one movement. She could feel herself expanding to accommodate his size and grasped his shoulders.

He retreated and plunged inside again. Anna could feel a deep pleasure building and opened herself fully to the experience. The sensations were so intense that she held onto him and tried not to lose her bearings.

She matched his rhythm and he devoured her mouth before moving on to her neck. She exploded into an orgasm and he followed, after one final thrust.

She lay next to him while their breathing returned to normal and he lightly ran his hand down her back.

Alistair left the bed for a moment to go into the bathroom and her heartbeat and breathing slowly returned to normal. He was incredibly sexy, so physical and tuned into her needs. She pulled the coverlet over her and watched him walk back to her completely unfazed by his nudity.

Pulling her into his arms, he softly kissed her neck and cheeks. "I have no words, Anna."

She held onto him, listening to his heartbeat. Sex

had never been like that for her. She'd had a couple of boyfriends after Sebastian, but each encounter was beyond awkward. She had thought something was wrong with her.

He tightened his arms around her. "I'm usually more controlled. I don't know why I couldn't hold on."

"I thought you were incredible." She kissed his shoulder.

Placing his hand behind her neck, he pulled her closer and captured her mouth with a seductive kiss. "No. But you're incredible."

"I can't believe that this is finally happening."

He ran a hand down her spine. "I'll make it more real this time."

"I think you already have." She watched him carefully and saw his boyish pride.

A few moments of silence passed between them and she snuggled against him, feeling everything was right with the world.

He began a slow seduction all over again and she became lost in his embraces, much later falling into a dreamless sleep.

***

The next morning when she was watching him dress, he told her, "I confronted Sebastian last week."

Panic began to build within her. She sat up and clutched the sheet to her. "Why would you do that?"

He sat next to her on the bed and traced the outline of her collarbone with his thumb. "I intended to destroy him, but backed off. He's found himself in the middle of a legal nightmare. He won't escape from it. This time they have a video of him blackmailing an ambassador's daughter."

She held her breath. "How did you find him?"

"He has an distinctive first name and he worked for Blackly Simonson. It wasn't that hard."

Looking off in the distance, she tried to make sense of his words. Why would he have gone behind her back?

He stood up and pulled on his shirt. "He was afraid of getting caught and had destroyed all of the evidence. I offered an obscene amount of money for the video of you, but he said it no longer existed. He was afraid of charges and only wanted extortion money, so he never sexually abused you. He had a friend, or so he says, take a video of you, but that was it."

Her spine became rigid. "He left me naked and drugged on a football field in the middle of the night. Anything could have happened to me."

Alistair watched her closely. "Luckily, it didn't. He's being fired from Blackly Simonson and has to deal with these new charges."

She looked away from him. "I don't completely trust him. The video could surface one day."

Alistair sat next to her on the bed and smoothed a strand of hair away from her face. "I'm sorry any of it happened. He's a horrible excuse for a human being. But, if he had the video, he would have sold it to me. "

She faced him, uncertain of whether she should be angry or not. She had dealt with Sebastian Fox and didn't need him to step in. "Did he act at all worried or remorseful?"

Standing up, Alistair continued getting dressed. "He barely showed any emotion. But if he had the video, he would have sold it to me. He did offer to sell me a drug so I could take my own video of you in a compromising position. He hasn't changed."

Taking a deep breath, she thought about the fact that Sebastian would finally have to face charges. If the charges stuck this time, it wouldn't be so easy for Sebastian to do it again to some other unsuspecting woman. A chill came over her, thinking back to that horrible time.

Alistair ran a hand through his hair. "He'll be made to account for his actions."

"I hope so. At this point, I want to move on and not think about him. I've wasted years trying to answer why he would have done that to me. I'm just ready to let it go."

He kissed her on the forehead. "I agree. Take a shower, and I'll meet you in the kitchen."

***

Alistair left her to shower and walked downstairs to the kitchen to make coffee. Looking out at the view, he rubbed the back of his neck and tried to clear his head of Sebastian Fox.

His anger wouldn't help in this situation. Anna needed to be able to talk about the incident. Sebastian had criminal intent, yet he didn't have any clue that other men would find his actions despicable. He must surround himself with like-minded individuals. Alistair relaxed his fists and decided to purge Sebastian Fox from his thoughts. With any luck, Anna would never have to set eyes on him again.

He took out two cups and used the coffee machine to brew a dark roasted blend. His housekeeper had set out a bowl of fruit on the table and he added scones that she kept in a bakery box.

Anna came into the room wearing the same dress from the day before with bare legs and her hair down.

He handed her a coffee. "I thought of visiting a few wineries today, first I can take you home to change or pack a bag."

She tucked a stray piece of hair behind her ear. "If I'm going to spend another night, I'll need a change of clothing."

He smiled. He'd much prefer to stay in, but something told him to spend time out in the world with her. She needed time to process what he had told her about Sebastian Fox. He turned away from her and tried to think of something boring or cold. His body was slow to cooperate.

And he needed time to adjust to the idea of getting involved with her. He would need to confront Fionn. Unfortunately, his best friend had made it more complicated. Fionn insisted that he keep away from Anna.

"Do you know which wineries you want to see?"

He placed his cup near the sink and didn't look at her. "Not particularly. I thought we could explore the area to the north of London."

He distracted her by having her look up different possibilities on the internet while he packed a lunch for them. His housekeeper always had the refrigerator well supplied with various foods. Locating an insulated bag in the pantry, he packed fruit, several cheeses, crackers, and olives. Next, he made two sandwiches with roast beef and lettuce.

Stepping outside, he turned to see that she was smiling at him. Leaning forward, he captured her mouth in a brief kiss.

"We should go before I drag you back inside."

She laughed openly, and he guided her to the car. Placing the lunch behind her seat, he waited for her climb in and then closed the door.

Walking around the car, he realized that spending time with her was testing his resolve. He couldn't remember being so hot for a woman. He had desired other women, but not with an all-encompassing longing where he had to force himself to do other things.

He could barely look at her. He wanted to trace her bare legs with his hands and explore her body fully. Putting the car into gear, he sped down the driveway.

"I found a wine tour that sounds interesting," Anna said.

The day passed in a blur. They stopped at her flat, toured a few wineries, and had a leisurely late lunch near a river before returning to his house.

When he pulled back into his driveway, she said, "I enjoyed the day."

He had kissed her several times that afternoon, but it hadn't been enough. "I enjoyed spending time with you."

She joined him on the steps and he pulled her into his arms. "I don't think that I'll ever get enough of you."

Anna laughed. "I hope you're right."

"I gave my housekeeper the night off."

Alistair guided her into the house and back to his bedroom. "I have plans for you."

She smiled at him, and he couldn't wait to remove her clothing.

***

Much later, Alistair held Anna until she fell into a light sleep. They had skipped dinner, but he wasn't hungry. He was much more focused on enjoying her. He closed his eyes and allowed himself to relax.

She stretched and pulled the sheet over her.

He rubbed her back. "Are you hungry? It's after nine o'clock and we skipped dinner."

She turned and faced him. "A little. But I can be distracted."

Kissing her briefly on the mouth, he said, "Let's go downstairs and eat something."

"Do you have a robe?"

He got out of bed. "We're completely alone."

Clutching the sheet to her, she said, "I don't walk around naked.'

"I'd like to make you something to eat while you sit around in the nude."

He thought she'd refuse, but instead she got out of bed. "If someone stops by, I'm going to murder you."

"Fair enough."

He watched her slowly walk down the main staircase and his body hardened in response. Maybe this wasn't such a great plan.

Keeping his back to her, he reached into the refrigerator and took out strawberries. "Would you like fruit and yogurt or chicken with salad?"

She perched on a stool. "Chicken with salad."

He assembled two plates while keeping his focus elsewhere.

"Should I make some dressing?" She climbed down from the stool and walked near him.

He reached out and grabbed her. Pulling her into his body, he said, "This wasn't a good idea. I can't think about food."

Anna placed a kiss on his chest and pushed away from him. "Certainly, a little nudity isn't going to stop you from eating?"

Mixing together oil and vinegar, she drizzled it over both plates.

He was going to lose his mind. "Anna."

She took a plate over the table and sat down. "I like eating while naked."

The breath in his chest stilled and he used every ounce of his control to reign in his rampant thoughts.

Sitting at the table across for her, he made himself take several bites of salad.

Anna looked at him. "Are you concerned about telling Olivia and Fionn that we're involved?"

He stopped eating for a moment. Fionn would lose his mind when he told him. "It's going to be a difficult conversation. Fionn feels that I'm not good enough for you."

Her gaze clouded. "He's worried that we want different things. It's not about you being good enough."

He shook his head. "Fionn knew me before I became a Martin. He knows all of the despicable details of my past." She had no idea where he came from or some of the things he did to survive.

"You were a young boy before you became a Martin. I can't imagine that your past is that terrible."

The easy atmosphere between them disappeared

in a flash. He didn't want to enlighten her, but the truth had to faced. Fionn would tell her at some point. Standing up, he gathered their plates and took them over to the sink.

She stepped behind him and glided her hands over his back. "Whatever sordid details you think are lurking in the shadows, I can tell you that I don't care. You told me weeks ago that the truth wouldn't shock you. It won't shock me either. I know life is complicated and bad things happen."

He shouldn't have allowed himself to travel down this path. He would only end up hurting her. He didn't want that to happen.

Turning around, he said, "I'll open a bottle of wine and we can talk upstairs."

She leaned up and pressed a kiss on his mouth. He gathered her in his arms and held her tightly for a few minutes.

He let her go and went in search of a bottle of wine. When he left Dublin, he left behind his past. He was given a new start at boarding school and his grandparents stayed with him each step of the way. They hadn't allowed him to take the easy way out. He had wanted to live up to the Martin name.

Stepping back into his bedroom, he saw Anna stretched out on the bed under the sheets.

He left the wine and glasses on the nightstand and went to look for briefs. There was no way he would talk about the past without some protection.

Pulling on boxers, he returned to the bedroom and poured wine for both of them.

Anna touched her glass to his and said, "To the truth and wherever that takes us."

He sat in a chair near the bed. "I have no idea where to start."

Taking a sip of wine, she said, "Fionn insists that you have no interest in long-term commitment. Why is that?"

Fionn didn't understand his need for independence or the cavalier way he lived his life at times. He had rebuilt the Martin legacy. That should be enough for his family.

"In my formative years, I lived in poverty with only my mother, and she worked all of the time. Most people would do whatever they could to survive. It wasn't until my grandparents' relationship that I began to see a different way. But that's not who I am. I'm a survivor at heart. I don't expect good fortune or happiness."

Anna bit her lip and then asked, "Why don't you expect happiness?"

His thoughts began to race. "We're getting off topic."

She sat up straighter and pulled the sheet against her breasts. "Somehow you think Fionn has an ironclad reason as to why we shouldn't date. What is that reason?"

The truth had to be faced. "He said to me on countless occasions that I treat women the same way that my father treated my mother, without respect or concern. I don't agree. I'm upfront and honest about my future plans and my ability to commit."

"If that is true, why does Fionn say that?"

He wanted to pace but stopped himself. "You're not the type of woman who seeks out a brief sexual encounter."

She turned her head to the side. "So this is about me, not you?"

He got up and placed his glass of wine down. "He questions my ability to show loyalty or commitment because underneath everything, he knows the truth about me. As a teenager, I stole things. I liked the challenge. I wouldn't listen and got even more daring. Until one day I crossed the wrong person. He burned down the apartment building I lived in with my mom and we lost everything."

Her expression froze. "That's a horrible lesson for a child."

He moved away from her. "I wasn't a child. I was thirteen."

"Thirteen is a child, Alistair." Anna got off the bed, still wrapped in a sheet. She stood in front of him. "If that's the best that Fionn can come up with then his objections are ridiculous."

He looked into her eyes. "Anna, it happened in the middle of the night and my mother and I barely got out. There were other flats affected."

She touched his arm. "This childhood incident has nothing to do with your capacity for commitment or loyalty. There were circumstances beyond your control that created the wrong environment for a bright, dynamic boy. You shouldn't allow that moment to define who you are."

His jaw became rigid. "It has. It serves as a reminder of what can happen if I fail to do the right thing. I knew stealing was wrong but I kept doing it."

She tipped her chin up. "Until you faced a hard truth and stopped the behavior. I bet you've never stolen anything ever again."

"No. I had to face the consequences of what happened, and nothing would compel me to go down that road again."

Anna wrapped her arms around him. "I'm sorry it happened."

She was too forgiving. He pushed her gently away. "Do you want to go home?"

Her blue eyes widened and she softly said, "I want you to make love to me."

Why wasn't she condemning him? He looked at her fully and didn't understand how she could simply accept his failings.

Unwrapping herself from the sheet, she let it fall to the floor.

He opened his arms and she stepped into his embrace. Her naked body ignited his desire and he couldn't imagine being with anyone else. He didn't understand why she wasn't horrified. He pushed aside his memories and set out to offer her every possible pleasure.

"I need you, love. All of you." He kissed her deeply and relished each sensation, each touch.

In the early hours of the morning, he ran his hand down her back and she woke up with a soft moan. He encouraged her response by gently stroking her breasts. He could feel his desire building as she kissed his jawline and he pulled her closer. Her body was warm and relaxed from sleep. He pushed aside the thought that he was becoming completely obsessed with her.

Chapter 8

A week later, Anna drove with him into London on a Thursday morning in insane traffic. She glanced at him and smiled to herself. They had spent a wonderful evening together, but he was going to be late for work again. She needed to figure out her own transportation if she continued staying at his house.

She thought about the coming weekend. Beatrice was turning six years old on Sunday and Olivia had invited all of her friends and family for a party. Their half-brother, William, was even planning on coming in from Ireland. She couldn't miss the party, and had pleaded with Elyse to cover a cosmetics launch. The client was known to be difficult and she hoped Elyse was up for the drama.

"You need to purchase a car or let me buy you one. I can't keep driving into the city before work."

"I agree," Anna glanced out the window, lost in thoughts about this weekend.

She was worried about attending a family event with Alistair. She hadn't told Olivia and Fionn that they were officially dating. Partly because Gala & More was insanely busy, but in part because she wasn't sure how long the relationship would last. Alistair had told her that he wasn't ready to settle down, and she had been careful not to crowd him.

"My flat doesn't have parking. I'm trying to locate to a reasonable flat near the new office space. After that, I can decide on whether to purchase a car."

Alistair stopped in the heavy traffic. "I can hire a car service to drive you around."

She shook her head. "We agreed to take things slowly. I should stay over less often."

Alistair said, "I don't see that as a solution."

"You can stay over at my place." Anna was busy sending emails from her phone.

His voice rose slightly. "You barely have running water."

She glanced up from her phone. "For someone who claims to be intimately aware of poverty, you have impossible standards."

They were stopped in bumper-to-bumper traffic. "Forget the flat. Buy a car and move in with me. The house has twelve bedrooms."

She kept her voice neutral, not daring to show the eruption of emotions his suggestion triggered. "What happens when you begin to feel fenced in?"

"I'm fenced in by London traffic."

Horns were blaring and Alistair maneuvered the car down a one-way street.

"Are you planning on going to Beatrice's birthday on Sunday?"

"There's a fifty-mile bike race that I committed to on that day. I can stop in after."

Nodding, she began to think about her day. Gala & More needed more staffing. "I have an event tonight. I'll be quite late, so I'll go back to my flat."

He pulled up to her office.

Anna reached over and kissed him. "I'm sorry I made you late again." She dashed out of the car and up the steps to her office. Before opening the door, she turned and caught sight of Alistair watching her. She waved and went inside.

He surprised her sometimes. For all of his speeches about not being fenced in, he was attentive and interested in her spending time with her and commuting together.

Katie and Elyse were working on boxing up the files and computers. Tomorrow movers were taking everything to the new office location.

Katie said over her shoulder, "Your sister called. She said your phone was switched off."

Walking into the conference room, she turned on her mobile and called her sister.

Olivia answered on the third ring. "Hi, stranger. The girls are missing you."

She felt horrible for avoiding them. "Work has been crazy, but I'm coming on Sunday."

"I'm looking forward to catching up. William will be here as well." After a slight pause, her sister asked, "How are things with Alistair?"

She smiled. "Did I tell you he invested into Gala & More and he selected us not only for the single event but also for all their event management for the next year?"

After a brief silence, Olivia said, "I thought as much. But I haven't heard about your personal relationship with him."

Instead of putting her sister off, she said, "We're dating and spending as much time together as we can. I haven't wanted to throw that in Fionn's face."

"Oh." She could tell her sister was choosing her words carefully. "Fionn has been concerned you would fall head-over-heels in love and that Alistair isn't into long-term. But you're an adult and can make your own decisions."

She didn't want to have to defend her relationship with Alistair. She understood that it was flawed. She wanted something steady and he wanted casual.

When she remained quiet, Olivia said, "Be careful, Anna. I know you've liked him for a long time and I don't want you to get hurt."

She wasn't planning on long-term. "Don't worry. I'm happy at the moment and I plan on taking it slow. But, I really need to get to work. I'll see you Sunday."

"Cheers."

Anna was glad she told her sister that they were dating, but she hoped Alistair didn't go to the party. Their relationship was too new, and she wanted to enjoy her time with Alistair without adding in family pressure.

The day absorbed all of her energy. They had two events on Saturday and she had to coordinate the move.

***

Alistair texted her late on Saturday night, suggesting that he pick her up. She responded with the address of the hotel. Gala & More had taken on a society wedding, and she'd cringed when she noticed her mother's name on the guest list.

Elizabeth approached her when the event was in full swing.

Anna barely embraced her mother, and the older woman stiffly pulled away. "Welcome back. I heard you were on a cruise."

Her mother shook her head and then said, "I was hoping you would have regained your sanity by the time I returned."

"No, I'm afraid that I haven't." Anna kept her shoulders relaxed and smiled slightly.

Elizabeth raised her chin. "I'd like you to come for brunch tomorrow."

"It's Beatrice's sixth birthday. I'm sure Olivia sent you an invite." It was surprising that Olivia tried to include her mother in every celebration, even though she never attended.

Her mother picked an imaginary piece of lint off of her dress. "I haven't gone through all of my correspondence yet, but I'll probably stay home."

She was impossible. "I'll call and maybe we can plan lunch for Wednesday."

Anna was interrupted with an event question and her mother walked away without another word.

Leaving the hotel at ten o'clock, Anna smiled when she saw Alistair waiting by his car. She dashed out in the light rain and threw herself into his embrace.

He held her tight for a moment. "You missed me."

Kissing her provocatively, he moved her away from the car enough to open the door for her.

Getting in the car himself, he said, "You need to hire more staff. You shouldn't be dealing with a wedding."

She buckled her seatbelt. "My mother was a guest and I thought she would implode."

He started the car. "I've met Elizabeth. Maybe two or three years ago. She reminded me of a tough old bird."

Anna smiled but looked away. That was an accurate description of her mother. She sometimes wondered what her father was thinking. But, then maybe he was attracted to strong, opinionated women.

Happiness surged through her. She wasn't expecting to see Alistair tonight. "How was your day?"

"I worked out and met a few friends for a game of golf."

She nodded. "Are you an amazing player?"

"I'd rather bike or play rugby, but I can play reasonably well." He let a moment pass before saying, "There is something that came up."

"Something good?" she asked in a teasing voice.

Alistair paused for a moment. "Not exactly. I stayed at the club for dinner and a woman I had been seeing on and off a few months ago ended up joining me. I bring it up because several photographs of us were taken at the restaurant."

Anna contemplated what she should say to him. "So if photographs weren't taken, you wouldn't have mentioned it?"

Alistair frowned. "It's not a big deal. Let's not let it become one."

She tried to hold back but couldn't. "So, you asked this woman to have dinner with you?"

His voice was low. "I did."

Anna remained quiet for a few minutes. "Why did you suggest picking me up tonight?"

"Why wouldn't I?" He kept his eyes on the road.

Her hands were trembling and she clenched them into tight fists. "If you would rather continue playing the field, don't let me stop you."

His calm voice soothed her nerves. "I had dated her a while ago, but our schedules hadn't lined up recently so I hadn't had the opportunity to tell her that I've been seeing you."

She bit down on her lower lip. "I'm not sure what I should say."

He hesitated for a brief moment, and then said, "She belongs to the private club and happened to see me at the bar."

Anna glanced at him and decided to take his explanation at face value. She needed to be careful and not let her past influence her relationship with him. She had to guard against turning every man into her father. Most men didn't cheat on their girlfriends, and certainly very few men led a double life. Images of her father and mother fighting brought her back to her childhood. Her father had cast her aside for his real family in New York, but it didn't explain why she had so many memories of her parents yelling at one another. Maybe she should ask William about it. Olivia knew very little about their father.

Her lungs constricted, making it hard to breathe. "I don't know why it bothers me. It shouldn't be a big deal."

***

Alistair disliked having to explain himself, but Anna had cause to feel distrustful. Her father had abandoned her in a very public way. It was gossiped about in certain circles; even today, it was talked about. But he couldn't solve the past for her. He had his own issues with his father refusing to acknowledge him. At least he had a loving mother; Anna didn't have that.

Either she would decide to put it behind her or she wouldn't. He couldn't change that for her, and he didn't want to spend his time trying to get her to see every man was not like Oliver Bolles. It'd be a wasted effort. She'd either move beyond her reluctance to trust others or she wouldn't.

When they arrived back at his house, Alistair considered telling her that he was worn out and suggesting sleeping in different rooms. But he resisted.

When he had picked her up earlier, she had thrown herself into his arms with such abandon that something had opened up deep inside of him. He cared about her. His heart had accelerated as he pulled her close.

Getting out of the car, he walked to her side and offered his hand. Anna wore a simple black dress with killer heels and he watched as she climbed out of the low vehicle. Her nearness and touch heated his desire for her. He pulled her towards him and captured her mouth in a passionate kiss. He could feel her clutch the front of his shirt and his desire increased.

He pulled away from her. "Let's go inside."

Closing the front door, he reached for her. "I gave the staff the night off."

She smiled at him. "You're clever and thoughtful."

Instead of slowly arousing her, he stripped her dress off of her and devoured her mouth. His hands explored her body fully, and when he was drenched with desire and she was encouraging each move, he plunged into her on the stairs. After several thrusts, she screamed with release and in one swift movement he

159

joined her.

He had unzipped his pants, and she was beautifully naked with clothing strewn between the doorway and the stairs. He kicked off his shoes and pants before carrying her up the stairs. He placed her on the bed and turned on the shower. Within seconds, she joined him in the bathroom and he kissed her. He was so fully aroused that he couldn't think.

When they finally made it to bed, Anna fell off to sleep without a word. He was surprised by the roughness in their physical connection tonight, but she had matched his desire at each turn and had even pushed him further.

Watching her sleep, he wondered if he was asking too much of her. He wanted her in his life, but he wasn't ready to commit fully. He needed to be able to work and travel without worrying about someone missing him or feeling neglected.

Anna turned over in her sleep and he tucked the sheet in around her body. She surprised him by being independent and a risk taker. At first, he had thought she was like her father, talented and intelligent but lacking in moral fiber. He had been unfair. She was nothing like Oliver Bolles. She had integrity and cared about the truth. She wasn't consumed by wealth or being part of a particular social class. Her shoddy flat and shifting careers attested to that. Maybe not having a connection with her father saved her.

The next morning after they had coffee in the kitchen, he called a car service and pulled her into his arms.

"I hope last night didn't put you off."

Kissing him on the lips, she said, "I enjoyed

every second. But it was a little challenging finding my clothing this morning."

"You need to leave some clothing here so you don't have to wear last night's dress."

He heard the car service beep.

She said, "I'll stop at my flat to change and then go over to Olivia's."

He opened the front door and watched her walk down the path.

She called back over her shoulder, "Good luck with the bike race."

He was becoming more and more captivated by her. He enjoyed figuring out how her mind worked, watching her embrace new challenges, and even the charming way she smiled at him. The issue was becoming that he couldn't find things about her that irritated or bored him. Usually a few weeks into a relationship, he knew what trait would cause him to end it. Maybe it was because she'd lived on in his imagination after the few stolen kisses in the garden. Over the years, he had attended social events at Fionn's and had tried to catch a glimpse of her, but she'd proved to be elusive.

He decided to tackle the fifty-mile bike ride and attempt to banish her from his thoughts. He would see her later in the day. He had spoken with Fionn on the phone, but hadn't seen him in person. The news that he was dating Anna had been accepted easily enough, but Fionn wasn't happy about it.

***

Anna, having showered and changed at her flat, had barely knocked on the door when Olivia pulled it open and said, "Thank goodness you're here. We need help."

Anna looked around the foyer. "Where are the girls?"

"Agnes is bathing them and then she will serve them an Irish tea upstairs so we can transform the garden." Olivia was lucky to have Agnes in her life. She was so much more than a guardian—Agnes was fully enmeshed in their lives and loved the girls as much as any grandmother would.

Anna followed her sister outside and took charge. A hundred pink balloons had been delivered in large clear bags and were tied to a lamppost. The linens sat stacked up on a bench, and the rented furniture was haphazardly placed around the garden.

She began to share her vision with Olivia and Fionn and then noticed William step out of the kitchen entrance. Anna let out a shriek. It had been months since she caught sight of her brother.

"Where have you been hiding?" Anna hugged him tightly.

He was eating an apple. "Here and there."

"Never mind. We have to get this party ready for our niece."

Within a few minutes, they had arranged the furniture and she was spreading the white linens over the tables. She instructed the men to add a weight to each balloon and scatter them in a haphazard pattern around the garden.

Olivia went inside to put together small gift bags. Anna placed pink flowers on each table and then organized the party games.

When Fionn went in search of the caterer, William asked, "So you're dating Alistair?"

"Yes. A little surprising, right?" Luckily, her brother accepted what she did without judgment.

William arranged the chairs. "How did that happen?"

Anna hung up an old-fashioned "Pin the tail on the donkey" poster on the fence. "We were thrown together in the events management company, and one thing led to another."

He teased her. "Yes, my mother mentioned that you left Blackly Simonson."

Anna stepped back and glanced around the garden. "Is she pleased to have me out of the family business or upset with the decision?"

"Maybe a little of both, but I wouldn't let it bother you. Diane has an odd fascination with wealth and social order."

It was odd to be discussing her stepmother. She had almost no contact with Diane Bolles. "What are your thoughts?"

His opinion mattered to her. "You should follow your passion. You're amazing with numbers, but maybe you needed a change."

Relaxing her shoulders, she said, "I like the challenge. Every day is different, and I'm able to take charge of building my own company. I don't think I could go back to working for someone else."

"You'll be successful. You have the drive and intelligence."

Fionn came outside with a tub of ice. "Will, can you bring out the beverages and place them in the ice?"

Anna went inside and helped Olivia with the gift bags, and then began arranging the flowers in the house.

Fionn joined her in the foyer. "So, I hear you're dragging Alistair here. He usually avoids children's birthday parties."

She looked at her brother-in-law. He and Alistair had been friends since their early childhood. Her heart plummeted. "I know you don't approve."

He stood facing her. "It's not about approval. He's not into long-term, and I've seen him break many hearts."

She didn't want to have this discussion. "Weren't you the same before Olivia?"

Fionn reached out and touched her shoulder. "You're thinking that what you have with him is different?"

Anna placed the vase of flowers she was holding on the round table in the foyer. "I don't know, Fionn. We're in the early stages of a relationship. So I'm not thinking about long-term right now. I'm launching a new career, which is challenging. But I like Alistair. A lot. Maybe too much."

Fionn cleared his throat. "He clearly is enchanted, but he'll disappoint you."

They were interrupted by someone knocking on the door. The guests began to arrive, most with small children in tow. Fionn greeted the guests and invited everyone inside.

Beatrice and Addy came downstairs and led the other children into the garden. The backyard looked like a magical fairyland with the decorations and a long birthday table with pink flowers and balloons. Even though the house was in the middle of London, they had a gorgeous backyard and garden.

A caterer had been hired and had set up in the kitchen. Everyone was served a lunch, and the adults were offered a glass of wine or bottle of ale. Anna helped with party games and leading the children in a scavenger hunt.

Alistair arrived towards the end of the party, and carried two large gifts wrapped in floral wrapping paper. After handing both Beatrice and Addy a wrapped present, he shook Fionn's hand before coming over and kissing Anna briefly on the mouth.

He had showered and changed into dress pants and a pressed light blue shirt. She asked him, "How was the fifty-mile race?"

"Challenging, but worth it." He smiled at her.

He watched her helping the little ones with a game, then retreated indoors to chat with Fionn.

Olivia came over and whispered to her, "I've finally found a way to entice Alistair to a child's birthday party: put you in charge of the children's games."

When the party began to wind down, she picked up Addy and held her. The little girl was exhausted and ready to crash. Fionn took her upstairs for a bath and an early bedtime.

After the last guest left, Anna sat with Olivia, William, Agnes, and Alistair in the front formal living room. They watched Beatrice play with her new dolls.

Fionn appeared with Addy, who had been bathed and put into her nightgown. He said, "She was too excited to fall asleep."

The little girl joined Beatrice on the floor and picked up a doll.

Fionn poured wine for the adults and spoke about

his recent travels.

The conversation moved to Gala & More, and Anna brought them up to date on the challenges.

Agnes asked, "Dear, wasn't there someone who was giving you a difficult time with the business?"

The room became silent for a moment. Anna said, "Agnes, Alistair was the person driving me insane, but he finally came around." Anna met his gaze and they broke out laughing.

Agnes clasped her hands together and said, "I'm sorry. I didn't mean to imply anything."

"It's fine," Anna said. "Alistair knows he was a tyrant."

Alistair smiled at Anna. "Or possibly someone may have been stubborn and reluctant to take much-needed advice."

Everyone laughed.

Olivia interrupted. "It's so interesting that the two of you have found each other. We should go out for a couple's night when our schedules line up."

Within a few minutes, Alistair suggested they leave, and Anna embraced her nieces.

After saying goodbye to everyone, Alistair placed his hand on her lower back and guided her out the front door.

"Did you find that awkward?" she asked him, stepping outside and closing the front door.

"Immensely." His voice was low. "Fionn is a good friend, but he is relentless. Yet Olivia seems happy about our relationship."

She glanced back at the house. "She's more of a romantic."

He stopped walking and pulled her into his arms.

"I can't get enough of you."

She kissed him. "Let's see what can be done about that."

***

The new space for Gala & More was located in a modern building on the second floor with access to a shared conference room. They collectively made the decision to donate their old office furniture and purchase new, modern furnishings.

Looking at the space, Anna couldn't believe that less than two months before she had walked into the cluttered and outdated office and had revamped it. This office suite had room for growth and was visually appealing. Katie now sat at a circular desk in a well-appointed reception area with a leather sectional and a glass wall and door overlooking the hallway and elevators. They had their business logo screened on the wall behind reception and everything had the same orange and cream tones.

Anna's office was spacious and placed among three offices that would eventually house Frances and a future hire. There were smaller side offices that Elyse and a new hire, Sam, inhabited.

Alastair stopped in with a huge display of flowers. She gave him a tour of the space. The team assembled on the sectional and they chatted for a few minutes.

"Gala has found the perfect location," Alistair said to everyone. They all agreed and enthusiastically talked about the new space.

Anna noticed that Katie and Elyse were much more committed to the company than when she had first met them. She couldn't believe she had considered firing them that first day. Now they were a positive influence on the business and reflected well on Gala.

Anna stood. "I have to get together a few items for the accounting service."

He met her gaze. "Do you have time for lunch?"

"Can you give me fifteen minutes to finish something?" Anna went to her office. The accounting service planned to be onsite once a week to reconcile their expenses and revenue, and she needed to organize paperwork for them.

Anna pulled on a lightweight coat and went in search of Alistair. He was chatting with Sam and Elyse.

It had been three days since she had seen him and she'd missed him. She tried to push away her longing and reminded herself to keep their conversation light.

He took her to an exclusive restaurant, and they were seated in a private alcove. The waiter handed each of them a menu.

"The new office is a good fit for Gala. You did an excellent job of finding the right space within budget."

Anna smiled and opened her menu. She decided on a salad with grilled halibut. Looking up, she found Alistair watching her.

"I'm traveling most of this week, but I wanted to discuss something with you."

Her chest tightened—he wanted to end their fling. She knew it would happen eventually and he had even warned her that he didn't seek out long-term relationships.

"You don't have to disclose your schedule, Alistair."

"I want to spend every waking moment with you, but your insane schedule and lack of a car are making it impossible." The warm tones of his voice soothed her ragged nerve endings.

She met his gaze and could tell he was trying to get a read on her. "I'm looking at a few flats this week. Two of them have parking, but in this area, I'll need to consider a roommate."

He leaned forward and softened his expression. "Move in with me."

Anna was stunned. "Why?"

He spoke in a neutral voice. "I miss you when you're not there."

Her shoulders were tight. "I can't do that, Alistair. Moving in is a commitment and I would want to know that our relationship is heading towards something long-lasting."

He rubbed the base of his neck. "You're practically living with me now. You spend at least four nights a week at the house, but the drive into London early in the morning isn't working. I barely get to work by nine o'clock and spend two hours in traffic."

Anna looked down at the place setting. "So you want me to move in so you don't have to drive me home in the morning?"

The waiter served their meal.

Alistair looked at her searchingly. "It's not about the drive, Anna. I want to walk into the house and know that you're there."

He seemed so earnest, but he hadn't said how he felt about her. She didn't want to turn him down, but there was no future in living with him. It'd lead to heartbreak at some point.

She shook her head. "We haven't been dating long enough to consider moving in together. It'd be smarter to take it slow and not live together. I'll find a flat with parking and look for a reliable car."

"That is your final answer?"

Anna wanted it to be different, but she wouldn't put herself in the role her mother had played for years. If she was going to commit to a relationship, she needed to know that her feelings were returned. She needed to be important to him.

She changed the subject to his vineyard and the upcoming event.

They finished their lunch and went outside. Alistair kissed her briefly on the lips before walking away.

The rest of the day passed in a blur as Anna pitched a new idea to a client, spoke with Frances, and then went over each detail about the upcoming wine launch for Martin Enterprises.

That night she texted Alistair, but he didn't respond. He hadn't told her where he was going, and he could be in a different time zone. She thought about her decision not to move in with him. She was falling in love and wanted to spend every possible minute with him. Maybe she shouldn't worry about the future, but the practical side of her didn't want to start thinking that he was interested in a permanent relationship. It would be a path to heartbreak.

The next day, she was pitching to a perfume company Olivia had recommended. She walked into their corporate offices and had a seat in reception. There was a tabloid opened to the society pages and she caught sight of Alistair in a photograph with a red-haired model.

Her stomach twisted. This must be the photograph he mentioned last week. There were three photographs showcasing Alistair and Brenda Waterman engaged in an intimate dinner. His eyes were glued to her and she was laughing.

The perfume manager interrupted her thoughts and said, "Alistair Martin is stunning. He is hot, brilliant, and everything he touches seems to turn to gold."

Anna closed the magazine and decided not to comment. She was in shock from seeing the actual photographs.

"The rumor is he's close to getting engaged," the woman said as if he were her best friend.

Could others see a side of Alistair that she had been denying? She was horrible with relationships. Maybe she was being overly optimistic. But he seemed so interested and attentive.

Her glimpse of the photographs clouded her thinking. Why did she let herself get involved with him? She had been warned and had a front-row seat to years of his dating. Even though she had attempted to avoid any contact with him in the past few years, occasionally she would catch a glimpse of him with a new girlfriend, usually a redhead.

Anna went through the motions of listening to the client and going over every aspect of the proposed work. Leaving the client, she pressed the button for the elevator and thought she might faint. She had barely taken in a full breath since seeing the photographs. She shouldn't care. Alistair had told her about the dinner and the reason for it. But seeing the images—and hearing the rumor of his impending engagement—brought a painful acknowledgment of the truth. He wasn't interested in long-term.

Instead of going back to work, she stopped in and saw Olivia at the design studio. The pace was frenetic; they were getting ready for fashion week in New York.

Olivia was talking with a young designer. Anna shouldn't have stopped in. She was holding back tears and should have gone for a walk instead.

"Anna, is everything okay?"

Olivia whisked her into her private office and closed the door. She threw her arms around Anna.

Anna wiped away a few tears and tried to gather her inner reserves.

"What happened? Is everything okay?" Olivia poured her a glass of water and motioned for her to sit.

She perched on the small, white sofa. "I went to a client meeting this morning and there was a tabloid opened on the table to the society pages." She paused for a moment. It was ridiculous to be so upset. "In the photographs, Alistair was having dinner with this beautiful model. He told me about the dinner, but actually seeing the images made it so much more real. It shouldn't upset me; we haven't made any promises to each other. But seeing the images cause me to doubt my relationship with him."

Olivia looked pensive. "Have a sip of water. It's good he told you about it. Maybe you should tell him how you are feeling about seeing the photographs?"

Anna placed the glass of water on the table in front of her. "No. It won't solve anything. It's my issue around trusting men, not his issue with commitment."

Olivia sat next to her. "You can't let our father and his mistakes taint your beliefs about men. Oliver made many mistakes in his life. But I know there are trustworthy, good men in the world. I believe you're capable of knowing the difference."

"I don't know. I find myself not trusting him, and it's not about who he is or how he lives his life. It's me."

Someone tapped on Olivia's door, and when her assistant popped her head in, Olivia said, "I need ten minutes." The assistant closed the door.

"I'm sorry. You must be terribly busy."

Olivia squeezed her hand. "It's fine. I always have time for you."

"Alistair seems happy at the moment, but I don't know how long it will last before he gets bored. The issue is that with every day that passes, I'm more and more drawn to him."

Olivia smiled. "Alistair seeks out adventure, but that doesn't mean he won't commit to a long-term relationship. I've known him a long time and I can tell something has shifted recently."

She didn't want to live in a fantasy world, expecting him to fall madly in love with her. "He lives in the moment, Liv. He asked me yesterday to move in with him. But he didn't talk about how he feels about me or the future." Anna sat up straighter and didn't allow herself to cry.

Olivia asked her gently, "How do you know how he feels if you're not willing to ask him?"

"I don't need to ask him. He enjoys the chemistry

between us but doesn't want to limit his freedom."

Olivia got up and handed her a box of tissues. "That may be a little unfair. I've never heard of Alistair living with someone. That's new."

She took a tissue and wiped her tears. "He's tired of driving to London. It would be more convenient for him."

Olivia laughed softly. "Do you expect me to believe that Alistair would choose convenience over freedom? He must be crazy about you and trying to figure out how to make the relationship work."

Her heart was shattering into a hundred pieces. "I don't know. He looked so happy in those photographs."

Olivia shook her head. "Photographs can be deceiving, and if the woman is a model, then she knows how to play to the camera."

Anna stood up. "I can't live with him without a commitment and an acknowledgment that he cares about me."

"Then the relationship will either stay the same or move forward."

Anna held off more tears. "Why do I feel heartbroken? I feel like I've already lost him."

Olivia looked sympathetic. "You're taking a stand. Either he'll meet your needs or he'll walk away."

She stood up. "It can be a little difficult to figure out how I'm feeling, especially since I know that he doesn't like to be fenced in."

Raising her voice slightly, Olivia said, "He may crave freedom or autonomy, but that doesn't mean you shouldn't tell him how you're feeling. He may surprise you."

"Thanks. You've cheered me up."

Olivia gave her another hug. "I've got to get back to work. It's chaos on the floor."

Anna looked at another flat that afternoon and ignored Alistair's call. She wasn't ready to speak with him.

Deciding to sign a lease for the next month, Anna took one last walk-through. She couldn't see herself living in the flat, but it was two blocks from the new office space and had parking. The neighborhood was an interesting mix of residential and shops. It was a one-bedroom flat with a spacious living area and beautiful windows.

She shook the estate agent's hand after signing the offer.

***

When Alistair returned that Friday evening, he picked her up at the office. Sam and Elyse were heading out to an event and she wished them success.

Anna locked the office and pushed the button for the elevator. Alistair ran his hand down her back and said, "I've missed you."

She turned into his embrace and kissed him briefly. "I can't believe that I have a Friday night off and that you're free."

The elevator opened and he took her hand when they stepped on.

Someone else stepped onto the elevator and she looked up at Alistair. "I'm surprised that you didn't have plans for tonight."

"I was planning on returning tomorrow, so tonight was left free. Do you want to have dinner in the city or head to my place?"

"Your place. Definitely. It's been a long week."

He drove out of the city and she asked, "How was your trip?"

He glanced at her. "Long. I'm used to traveling frequently, but somehow it's getting harder to leave you."

Her heart accelerated. She smiled at him and ran a hand down his thigh.

She told him, "I found a flat two blocks from my office with parking."

He kept his eyes on the traffic. "I thought we were going to revisit your living arrangements."

His comment surprised her. She had assumed that he would want to keep some distance between them. He had told her at the beginning of their relationship that he didn't want to be trapped or fenced in. Had he changed his mind?

Anna shrugged. "For now, it's better if we maintain separate residences." Anna tried to lighten the conversation. "I'll purchase a car and when you're traveling, I'll stay at the flat."

His voice held no emotion. "We could have discussed getting a flat that would work for both of us and splitting our time between two residences."

She removed her hand from his leg and crossed her arms. "You can stay over whenever you like. I'm crazy about you and want to spend as much time together as possible. But we both have demanding work lives."

Alistair changed the subject to acquiring a new vineyard and asked about her week at Gala. She discussed the current activities at the company and upcoming events.

She looked forward to seeing him and missed him when he was away. But she reminded herself to not fall too deeply for him.

***

He could tell when she distanced herself. She became quiet and physically pulled back from him. Maybe she didn't want to live with him? They hadn't been dating for that long, but he thought their relationship had deepened enough that she would want to spend more time together. Maybe she needed more of a commitment from him.

"Has something happened this week to upset you, love?" She would tell him if there was something.

She looked out the window. "It's not very important, and I'm not even sure why it bothered me."

"Tell me." He was curious now.

She stared down at her hands. "It's nothing. I happened to be at a client meeting and a tabloid was open to the society pages."

"Ah. You saw the photographs from the dinner I had with Brenda."

She nodded and remained quiet. Why would it upset her? He had told her that it was a possibility, so it shouldn't have come as a surprise.

"Why did seeing a few images of me having dinner upset you?"

"You looked happy. I guess I felt left out in some odd way. I know it doesn't make any sense."

He shifted into a higher gear. "Emotions don't always make sense. I'm sorry you were upset. I wasn't particularly joyful that evening, but I thought it was the right thing to do."

"I understand. Forget I said anything."

He thought about her childhood. He understood feeling left out. Even now, when his grandparents talked about his father, he felt slighted in some way or overlooked. He could only imagine that she would feel the same about a father who left her for his proper family.

"I don't plan on any future encounters with Brenda."

She smiled at him. Hopefully, they would be able to have an enjoyable evening. He had asked his housekeeper to prepare a special meal and he planned to take her to a shop in the morning to get fitted for a road bike.

He drove up his driveway and parked near the garage. Leaning over, he kissed her before they got out of the car.

He never tired of watching her climb out of his car in heels and a short dress.

"I have a surprise for you."

They walked arm in arm to the house. "I ordered a road bike for you from a local shop. I thought we could go in the morning and check the fit."

She looked at him. "I can't possible keep up with you."

She was in amazing shape and, with some endurance training, she could handle an intermediate course. "There are a couple of upcoming trips that I wanted to take you on, but you'll need some riding experience first."

He had never taken a girlfriend cycling. He gravitated to all-male adventures, but something was shifting. He wanted to experience a cycling trip with her.

"I don't have that much experience."

"It's fine." He opened the front door. "If after a few outings, if you don't like biking, you can opt out."

"I'd love to give it a try. Thank you."

He kissed her briefly and then said, "I called ahead and asked for a special meal to be prepared, so we'll need to eat first."

He called out to his housekeeper, Helen.

She had set up an elaborate table on the terrace and had prepared Beef Wellington.

Opening a bottle of merlot, he watched Anna greet Helen and thank her for cooking the meal.

They sat down at the table and he could only think about getting her alone. He watched her look at the wine.

"May your glass be ever full." She lightly tapped her glass to his.

The conversation moved from his vineyard to road biking. He described the different routes in Spain and Ireland that he had biked.

"I'll have more flexibility in the fall, when Frances comes back part-time."

"Sounds like she's enjoying motherhood. You may need a back-up plan."

The housekeeper cleared the plates and offered dessert.

Anna shook her head and he thanked Helen for the lovely meal.

"It's true. She wants to be involved, but she's enjoying her daughter."

She was brilliant and talented. "Are you losing interest in Gala & More now that the challenge is behind you?" Her energy and drive would push the company forward.

She laughed. "I don't think the challenge is behind me yet. Have you seen the balance sheet for this month?"

"True. I guess we'll see when you hit the one-year mark."

She was twenty-five and fully immersed in her second career. He wondered what she would decide to take on next. He asked her, "Do you want to take a walk in the garden?"

"No." Anna stood and waited for him.

He smiled at her. She had read his mind. He had every intention of wearing her out. He couldn't wait to strip her dress off of her and take her in the shower, and then again on the bed.

Chapter 9

Anna smiled at the head librarian and motioned for the caterer to begin serving tea. The formal event was being held outside and the weather was cooperating. The large London library was celebrating a hundred years of service with poetry readings, classical music, and children's activities.

She watched a pregnant woman accept a cup of tea. The woman was glowing with happiness, and an inkling of worry skittered over Anna's composure. Her period was nearly a week late. She had purposely put it out of her mind, but now, seeing a woman about to go into labor, made her think about scheduling a doctor's appointment.

Katie interrupted her thoughts. "This came together well."

She smiled. "It's a special event." She couldn't think about a possible pregnancy right now. They had been careful and their relationship was too new to deal with more complexity.

"I can handle the teardown if you want to go. I know you have some things to finish for the Martin event."

Looking at Katie, she smiled and said, "Thank you. Text me if anything comes up."

She thought about checking on Elyse and Sam, who were overseeing a fiftieth-anniversary party, but decided to head back to the office to go over Alistair's event for next weekend. She had already confirmed the details with his staff, but decided to go through everything again. She wanted it to be flawless.

Within twenty minutes, she unlocked the door to Gala & More and stepped into the quiet space. She locked the door behind her and went to her private office. She called Frances and they discussed the menu again. After getting off the call, she phoned her doctor and made an appointment.

Hearing the buzzer ring at the main door, Anna walked into the foyer and noticed that a delivery person was waiting with a bouquet of flowers. Opening the door, she accepted the pink roses and signed the electronic delivery slip.

Alistair was traveling, but he must have had his assistant send her flowers. She thanked the delivery person and walked back into the reception area. Opening the small white card, she read, Meet me at five o'clock at Tack & Tavern.

They hadn't spent much time at Alistair's microbreweries. He preferred to spend time at home or go to sporting events. She had assumed that it felt too much like work. But why did he want to meet her there tonight? It was odd, but she placed the card down and went back to work.

In some ways, she wanted to visit her doctor before seeing Alistair. Why worry him if she was just late? She had been under a considerable amount of stress launching the company; couldn't that have put off her cycle? She did need to go on birth control instead of just relying on condoms.

Heading out at nearly five o'clock, she decided to share her concerns with Alistair instead of keeping the worry to herself. He wouldn't be happy, but at least he would know what was happening. Deciding to get a taxi, she gave the name of the brewery, Tack & Tavern, to the driver.

Stepping onto the curb, she realized she was dressed more for a fancy library event than a pub. Her sleeveless blue linen A-line dress was slightly creased but fit her perfectly. She removed her small white sweater and tucked it into her leather handbag.

A man opened the door for her and she stepped into the brewery. It was a large open space with brick walls and, behind a glass divide, there were large brewery tanks. Her gaze swept the bar area, but she didn't see Alistair.

"So you came," a male voice said from behind her, and a chill ran up her spine.

Turning around, she saw Sebastian smirking at her. She had caught sight of him at Blackly Simonson a few months ago, but hadn't spoken to him in years. He made her skin crawl.

Anna narrowed her eyes. "You had flowers sent to my office?"

Sebastian stepped off to the side. "It seemed the easiest way for us to have a chat."

She stayed in the middle of the foyer. "I have nothing to say to you."

He raised his voice fractionally. "Your boyfriend seems to think that you are concerned about our association."

"He's wrong. I'm not interested in the slightest."

There was no way that she would show fear or anxiety in front of him.

He shrugged. "You're afraid to have a conversation with me?"

"I'm not afraid, just unwilling." She looked around the space and considered her next move. She didn't want to go back out onto the street in case he followed her, but staying in the same place with Sebastian was also not an option.

"I'll make it brief."

Did he have an accomplice here? She pulled out her phone and texted Alistair. She hoped he was in the country, or at the very least that his manager would come to her aid.

She moved out of the flow of patrons and stood next to the table, waiting for him to say something.

"I'll make you a deal." His aristocratic looks were still intact. It probably helped him deceive others.

She glared at him, "I don't negotiate with criminals, Sebastian. You should know that by now."

His smirk widened. "Yes, but you have become rather cozy with Frances Casey as of late. Even going as far as going into partnership."

Her eyes narrowed. "I don't see how that can be any concern of yours."

His hand gestured dismissively. "She was desperate to get her hands on the photographs of her sister." He had no regard for anyone but himself.

Anna crossed her arms. "What can you possibly gain from approaching me?"

Worry crossed over his features but was quickly replaced with arrogance. "I need my position with Blackly Simonson. A positive word from you would go a long way."

She took a slight step backwards. "I'll not help you. You've broken the law countless times. I was surprised that they hired you."

He turned his hands over and faced his palms towards her. "I was just a college kid when that happened. I've left those activities behind."

She shook her head. "Then why would Blackly Simonson dismiss you? Something criminal must have come up."

He kept his voice low and menacing. "If you help me, I'll make sure that the Casey girl gets all of her original photographs back."

"Unless it's evidence that the Casey family can use to press charges, I'm not interested."

His lips tightened. "There are plenty of photographs of us together. Do you want your name dragged down with mine?"

Anna shrugged. "Put them out there, Sebastian. So I dated a sleazy guy when I was young and didn't know better."

Sebastian pointed at her and leaned closer. "I doubt your boyfriend would want the bad press. He would probably end the relationship. Is it really that difficult to make one call?"

She needed to find an exit strategy. The pub was getting more crowded and he probably had someone with him.

"You're a creep. I hope you get what you deserve."

Sebastian grabbed her arm painfully. "Lower your voice. This doesn't have to get nasty."

He let her go and stepped back. Glancing over her

shoulder, she saw Alistair, who immediately wrapped his arms around her. "If you come into this establishment again or approach Anna for any reason, I'll have you arrested," he said to Sebastian.

She watched in fascination as Sebastian took money out of his wallet, put it on the table, and left the pub.

Alistair turned her to face him and gathered her closer, whispering, "Are you okay?"

She nodded. "Yes. Surprisingly, I am. He wasn't able to push me around the way he could when I was nineteen. He tried to convince me to put in a good word for him at Blackly Simonson."

Alistair held her tightly. "I don't trust him. I'm relieved that you are okay, but we need to think about security for a period of time."

Leaving the pub, Alistair said, "I don't want you to return to your flat. Sebastian could easily approach you there."

Anna ran her hands up and down her upper arms. "I'm moving to my new flat next week and I can stay with Olivia until then."

He put his arms around her. "Stay with me."

"I can't let Sebastian rattle me; then he will have won. I can't imagine he would try anything desperate."

"Never underestimate a man who's cornered. Especially one who is lacking in any moral fiber."

***

Anna was deep in thought on the drive out of London. He needed to find a way to protect her. Sebastian was a criminal, and the less he had to lose the more dangerous he became. How could he make her understand that it wasn't weak to take precautions?

He kept his tone neutral. "Why did you agree to meet him?"

"I was at work this afternoon and a florist delivered flowers with a note to meet at your brewery."

He glanced at her. "You thought the message was from me?"

She twisted a ring on her finger. "Yes. I can't imagine how Sebastian could think that I would help him after everything he did."

Alistair shifted the car and changed lanes. "He must be desperate." He glanced at her, "You need to take extra precautions and not become too accessible."

She met his gaze. "As an events person, I'm constantly out in public. It can't be that hard to figure out where Gala & More will be."

Touching her knee, he said, "We can hire security."

Anna looked down. "I have something that I need to tell you. But I'd rather wait until we are back at your place."

His shoulder muscles tensed. Was there something else that Sebastian threatened her with? Alistair put on the radio for the remainder of the drive and tried to unwind. He needed to be rational if he was going to protect her. He couldn't allow himself to be overcome with fear.

Helping her from the car, they walked up the pathway holding each other.

The sun hung low in the sky and cast an orange haze over the valley. He kissed her before opening the front door.

"Do you want to have a glass of wine out on the

terrace?"

She nodded. "Sure."

He watched her pale considerably as he poured them a glass of wine. Whatever was on her mind, it worried her and she was reluctant to disclose it.

Her hands clenched into fists and then straightened out. He had a sense that he wouldn't like what she had to say.

He handed her a glass of merlot. "This is a new blend." He pulled out a chair and sat next to her at the outdoor table.

Anna wet her lips and placed the glass of wine on the table. "I don't want to make a huge deal of this, but my period is a week late and I plan on seeing my doctor on Monday."

He doubted she was pregnant. They had been careful and had only been together for a few weeks.

He placed his glass down. "You've had the week from hell. Moving your business, dealing with Sebastian, and now this."

Her expression was pained. "I'm hoping that it's nothing and then I'll go on birth control."

"Whatever it is, love, we'll make it work." He pulled her into his lap and could feel her heart beating excessively.

"I'm worried." She relaxed into his embrace.

"I see that. There is no sense in worrying until we have all the facts. There are probably a million reasons for your period to be late." He was waiting for a feeling of panic to overtake him, but nothing happened. The idea of her being pregnant didn't rattle him. How was that possible?

She moved away slightly to look into his eyes. "I

can't believe that you aren't more freaked out."

He ran his hand up her back. "I'm an adult. I'm aware that there are potential consequences to having sex."

In fact, his body was craving her right now. It'd be insensitive to encourage her to have sex, but it was all he could think about. He had missed her and ended his travel a day early to see her.

He needed a distraction. Maybe he should work for a couple of hours and suggest that she relax in the tub and rest? She had been through the mill today.

"You seem preoccupied."

"Maybe you should relax and take a bath. I'll do some work."

She stroked her hands down his arms while pushing against him and kissing his neck. "I'd rather you offer me a distraction."

He gently distanced himself. "You've had a difficult day."

"I need you, Alistair."

He kissed her. He was ready to strip her naked out on the terrace, but instead he led her upstairs.

With each passing day, he was becoming more and more obsessed with her. He couldn't wait to see her, and when he did, his heart constricted. He was losing control. Had he finally found love?

Chapter 10

She and Alistair left her doctor's office on that Monday armed with a prescription for birth control pills and an admonishment for her to slow down and get some rest. A blood test had confirmed that she was not pregnant, but for some reason, she didn't feel overjoyed.

Pressing her fingers to her temple, she tried to make sense of her reaction.

Instead of pushing the button for the elevator, Alistair gathered her into his arms. "It's better if we plan ahead for a pregnancy, but I'm sure we would have made it work brilliantly."

Smiling at his uncanny ability to read her mind, she put her head on his chest. They were in the early days of a relationship and should be relieved.

The elevator doors opened a pregnant woman got off.

They stepped on and after the doors closed, she said, "I'm not ready for that."

He laughed and said, "I'd like you to meet my mother before the event this weekend. Can you drive down to the vineyard with me on Wednesday?"

Anna glanced at her phone. "There are so many details that I should check on this week. Can I meet her when she comes to London?"

He pulled her into an embrace and kissed her forehead. "It's fine."

She met his gaze. "This is my first solo event. It's important that it comes together flawlessly. Going away for a day or two will just add pressure."

He double-parked so he could let her off close to her office. "Do you want me to pick you up tonight after the art opening?"

She kissed him and he pulled her towards him for another lingering kiss. "Olivia is coming to the opening and I made plans to go home with her. I haven't spent much time with my nieces."

Anna climbed out of the car, but before she closed the door, he said, "If you're sure, then I'll head down to the vineyard today. I've been neglecting the place since my obsession with you has taken over."

She smiled. "Go ahead. I'll see you at the end of the week."

"Don't let your guard down. Sebastian is out there. You should use the security service I hired and not go back to your flat alone."

Closing the door, she waved and made herself go into her office building. She didn't want to have a security professional following her every move, but she wasn't willing to make herself an easy target for Sebastian either.

Going through the motions of her day, she returned messages, checked her email, and then took a new client to lunch. Frances came in with the baby in the afternoon and the entire office took a break. Anna and Frances decided to take a drive out to the venue for Martin Enterprises and Katie promised to watch over the napping baby.

Frances drove and reminded Anna that the planning had been extensive—much more than most of their events.

"Yes, but Alistair is also our investor and the event is different. Martin Enterprises hosted it in the past in hotels or breweries."

Frances smiled at her. "He's in love with you. You could serve old cheese and wine in paper cups and he would be fine."

Her partner's flippant attitude added to her stress. She refused to use her relationship with Alistair to smooth over a mediocre event. "No, he wouldn't. He can be insane about work. This needs to reflect well on Gala & More."

They walked through the elaborate gardens and Frances looked at the spot for the tent. "It's going to be magnificent. You need to stop worrying."

Anna took in a calming breath. "I hope so, but until everything comes together and guests begin arriving, it's difficult to know if it'll be successful."

"I've learned over time that as long as all the basic elements are right, even small hiccups during the event won't negatively affect the outcome. Stay calm and handle whatever comes up."

She looked at Frances. Stressing over the event wasn't going to help. She decided on this career path and needed to find the joy in putting together events.

Anna tried to relax her tight body. "You're right. I'm sorry if I've been stressed out over this."

"I wouldn't have chosen anyone else as a partner, Anna. You are brilliant with numbers, a strong negotiator, and you know how to put together a social event."

***

Anna didn't sleep the night before the event. It didn't help that Olivia had convinced her to stay the week at her house and Beatrice insisted on sleeping in the guest room with her. She adored her little niece, but woke up with a stiff neck from hanging off the bed.

She got out of the house before anyone was awake. After stopping for a coffee at her new favorite café, she was the first person at the office.

Elyse came in an hour later and stopped in her office. "So, are you ready? Today is the big day."

Anna placed a few files in her bag. "I can't wait until it comes together. I'm going to head out soon and watch the tent get put up."

Elyse raised her eyebrows. "You should probably go to the spa for the day and let us handle it."

She shook her head. "I don't think I could relax. I'm on edge. I got my period today and feel like hibernating with a hot mug of tea."

Elyse leaned against the doorframe. "Have you heard from Alistair?"

Anna leaned back in her chair. "He's returning from the vineyard today. Apparently he had a few unexpected guests this week and couldn't get back yesterday."

They talked for a few more minutes about other clients and Anna gathered her phone and bag.

"Wish me luck."

"You won't need it. I'll come around four o'clock. Just text if you need anything before then."

Anna took the rental van that had been stocked

the day before with everything that was needed and headed to the public garden. The executive director was on site and looked happy to see her.

She climbed out of the van and went over to the older gentleman.

His eyes sparkled. "Anna, I'm so thrilled all of this worked out. From this one night, we have closed our budget gap for the year. And with so many people attending, I'm hoping for another event here soon."

Smiling, she said, "I'm thrilled as well. I think everyone will enjoy the evening."

The day passed in a blur of activity as numerous vendors came in and got the space ready for two hundred guests. The temporary lighting that was hung throughout the gardens was spectacular. The only worry Anna had was the caterer. Even though they specialized in outdoor affairs, she hoped the food would be delicious. They had to contend with limited water and electricity, not to mention insects and flies.

The head chef seemed organized and confident, so now she had to take it on faith that they knew what they were doing.

Alistair appeared an hour before the guests began arriving. She was kept busy, but caught sight of him several times.

She had asked him to keep their relationship low-key in front of her staff, but she wanted to throw herself into his arms. They hadn't seen each other all week and they were both taken up with last minute questions.

Alistair's sales team arrived and they asked to make a few slight changes.

Just before the event was set to start, she made

her way over to a staging tent and changed into an evening dress. Her sister had opened up her showroom and allowed her to pick whatever she wanted. She chose a black lace cocktail dress with an unlined yoke at the neckline and exquisitely detailed sheer embroidered tulle in small stripes throughout the skirt. It fit perfectly and was both striking and stylish.

Alistair pulled her into an embrace on her walk back to the event area.

He kissed her neck. "You're gorgeous tonight."

Stepping back, she glanced at his formal suit. "You look amazing yourself."

He smiled at her. "This event will reflect well on my company, as well as yours."

She kept her tone light. "That's the goal."

His eyes searched her face. "I need to talk with you about something, but we can leave it for later."

"Is something wrong?" she asked.

He kissed her lightly on the mouth. "Not exactly, but it is complicated. It's not worth discussing right now. We should greet guests."

Anna went in search of the servers and attendants. She had thought about her typical role at an event, staying behind the scenes and making it all work. But with dating Alistair, it was more complicated. He wanted her at his side, greeting guests and meeting his friends.

The sun had started to set and several well-dressed guests arrived. She watched the women walk along the fabric-covered path in heels and everything seemed fine. The tent had been set up by the grapevines on an old foundation. The stonework, along with the lanterns, created an atmosphere of both nature and history.

Fionn and Olivia had arrived and were speaking with Alistair and a group of wine fanatics. Many of the people who were attending tonight bought large quantities of wine for their restaurants and hotel chains.

There was a well-coordinated effort to encourage everyone to sample different varieties of wine while the wait staff walked around with trays of hors d'oeuvres. She could hear laughter and snatches of conversations coming from many directions.

A tall redhead arrived, and Anna instantly recognized her. Brenda Waterman. Her long, straight red hair hung down to her waist and her skimpy dress barely concealed her breasts. Brenda made her way to Alistair and hung on his arm. Anna felt her stomach clench.

Making eye contact with Alistair, she raised her glass to him and then took a sip. He removed Brenda from his arm and greeted a couple waiting to speak with him.

The event moved to speeches and the dinner. The tables looked spectacular, with rustic floral arrangements and specialty lighting.

Anna joined Olivia and Fionn at their table and listened to Alistair start the evening with a prediction for the coming harvest. He spoke about the international pressures on vineyards and the reputation of the U.K. in the burgeoning marketplace. His speech was polished and entertaining and Anna breathed a sigh of relief. The event was a success.

When he turned over the microphone to his marketing vice president, Olivia whispered, "He has single-handedly revived the industry."

"He had something unexpected come up at the vineyard."

Olivia nodded. "His mother visited and she's here tonight. Have you met her?"

Anna shook her head. The next speech began and she lost the opportunity to speak with Olivia.

The dinner was divine. The caterer had been a good choice. She watched the guests for signs of discomfort, but everyone was drinking and socializing. The quintet she'd hired played classical music on a small terrace above the tent and added just enough interest to the evening.

Anna went in search of Alistair. He wasn't in the tent any longer, and she checked the area where the wine tasting had been set up. She caught sight of him in the lower part of the garden having a conversation with Brenda. He didn't look pleased but listened intently to whatever the woman was saying to him.

She retraced her steps. He would come and find her at some point. Her mind raced through different possibilities.

Coming across an older woman standing alone on the path, Anna smiled politely.

The woman pressed her lips together before saying, "You must be the Bolles girl."

She held her hand out and said, "Yes. I'm Anna Bolles."

The woman briefly touched her hand and smiled. "I'm Deirdre, Alistair's mother."

Anna kept her tone friendly. "It's quite nice to meet you."

His mother frowned. "I'm afraid I don't share the

same good feeling. You see, I'm rather fond of Brenda and was sorry to hear that you have come between her and Alistair. They were to be married later this year."

A slight chill ran from her neck down her back. The tabloids had speculated about a possible engagement, but Alistair had said nothing.

"I guess it's somewhat natural because you grew up with an odd arrangement. But I had hoped for more for my only son. He has found so much success in the business world, he needs to have a wife and family."

She tried to keep her voice neutral as an intense pain swept through her body. "He wasn't seeing anyone when we started dating."

"I just spoke with him last week and he told me that he planned on proposing tonight."

Anna stepped back. "That can't be true. You must have misunderstood."

Her voice became shrill. "There is no misunderstanding. He told me."

Brenda came up the walkway alone and greeted Deirdre.

Anna nodded at the two of them and walked back to where she had seen Alistair. He was looking out at the view over the gardens.

"I met your mother."

He turned towards her and he looked pensive. "I'm sorry. I should have introduced you, but she has been acting a little odd tonight."

Anna folded her arms across her chest. "Yes. She seemed to think that you were about to propose to Brenda."

He met her gaze. "I think the two of them have encouraged each other's fantasies."

She bit her lower lip. "Why is she even here?"

He stepped closer to her. "Brenda is a model and has an account with a large lobby for the Wine Growers' Association. In fact, they were filming at my vineyard this week."

Anna shook her head to clear her thoughts. A painful lump in her throat formed. "Why didn't you tell me?"

Alistair held up his hands. "I had forgotten that a shoot was scheduled. If you remember, I invited you down to meet my mother this week."

Her mind was trying to make sense of the events over the last week. Why did his mother think they were going to get engaged? "Your mother is fond of Brenda."

He touched her shoulders. "She has been modeling for the association for a number of years. Everyone within the industry knows her."

She stepped away from him. "I can see why your mother is keen on the association. You're the most sought-after vineyard owner in the U.K. and she is the representation of all that is good about the industry."

"You are making too much of this."

Pain engulfed her. "You spent the week with her at your vineyard."

Alistair stepped closer to her. "There was filming, but I barely had any interaction with her. As far as I'm concerned, I let her have her say at the dinner weeks ago and have moved on."

She lifted her chin. "Why does your mother think that I've come between you and her?"

His voice rose and he made a sweeping gesture with his hand. "I don't know why she is acting the way she is. I think Brenda spoke with her after I ended the relationship, giving her some sort of false hope. I'll speak with her."

She didn't want to deal with his mother again this evening. She wanted to escape the situation entirely. "In that case, I shouldn't come home with you. It would be too awkward."

He ran a hand through his hair and then stepped away from her. "I'm sorry, Anna. It was such a spectacular event and I hate that it's ending this way."

She could feel tears forming in her eyes. "It's fine. There will be a ton to do to tear down the event and you should go and spend time with your mother."

He pulled her into his arms. "I can't imagine that it will be that difficult to straighten out."

"I should get back and check on everything." She pulled away after giving him a brief kiss and headed back to the tent area.

The party was beginning to wind down and she immersed herself in the teardown and cleanup tasks.

By the time she climbed into the hired car, Anna was exhausted. She gave her new address to the driver and hoped that the moving company placed her belongings in her flat today. She had planned to stay at Alistair's house this weekend and hadn't thought about unpacking.

It was hours later when she located sheets in one of the boxes and made her bed. She curled up into a ball and let her tears flow. Anna couldn't believe how horrible Alistair's mother had been. There was a small part of her that hoped that Alistair would come and check on her.

She was in love with him. But it seemed that she

was not destined to have a good relationship with his mother. It shouldn't surprise her. Her own mother was tricky at best.

Replaying the scene in her head, she wondered if his mother was right. Maybe Brenda Waterman had expected Alistair to propose to her. Fionn had warned her that Alistair left a trail of broken hearts. Her experience of Alistair was so different than how Fionn thought of him. Did she have blinders on and only wanted to see what she wanted?

Anna was at a disadvantage in relationships with men. She didn't have a good example to reference. Her father had let her down countless times. It was only in the last several years that she was able to have a healthy, adult relationship with Fionn and William. Besides them, she had had a few casual boyfriends, but it would always end before getting too serious. Why did she see Alistair so differently than everyone else did? Could she be wrong about him? She had thought they were becoming more serious, but she hadn't wanted to crowd him. Maybe he was pulling back and she hadn't recognized it?

Chapter 11

Anna dressed in a pale yellow A-line dress for brunch with Alistair and his mother, Deirdre. She had reluctantly agreed to go when Alistair called her last night, but wasn't looking forward to it. Applying a small amount of makeup, she replayed the conversation in her head with Alistair's mother yesterday.

The doorbell chimed and, opening the door, she was surprised that they had both come upstairs instead of texting her to come down. Her eyes raked over Alistair and her body nearly dissolved. In a few short hours, she had forgotten how gorgeous he was and how much she missed him. Stepping back instead of kissing him, she invited them in.

Her gaze clashed with his. "I must apologize. I'm in the process of moving in. I didn't know you were coming upstairs."

Deirdre spoke first. "It's my fault. I wanted a moment alone with you to apologize. It wasn't my intention to cause a problem between you and my son. I misunderstood his intentions."

Anna fidgeted with her handbag. "It's fine. We should forget it happened."

Alistair held out his hand and Anna placed her

hand in his. Pulling her lightly forward, he kissed her cheek. "There is a wonderful place around the corner to get brunch."

They all walked to the elevator and Anna thought she saw a look of irritation come over Deirdre. Alistair meant well, but his mother was going to resent his high-handedness. She resolved to try and put the older woman at ease and begin to repair the damage that was caused.

Stepping away from Alistair, Anna asked, "Do you get to London often?"

Her lips pressed together, and then she said, "Luckily for you, dear, I rarely leave Dublin."

"I hope Alistair and I are able to come and visit you. I love spending time in Dublin."

Anna kept the dialog going through the brunch by talking about Gala and More and then Olivia's girls. She attempted to make a connection through Fionn, but apparently Deirdre didn't care very much for him.

When they finally said goodbye outside her building, Anna was relieved. She stepped forward, embracing Deirdre in a stiff hug and wished her well.

Alistair kissed her on the lips and mentioned that he would stop over later in the evening.

She spent the entire day working on her new flat and tried to unpack every box. She obsessed about Brenda. She couldn't understand why the model was able to create such a divide between her and Alistair. Maybe it was because she was a model and intent on getting her way? Brenda also had his mother's full approval. It shouldn't matter to her, but somehow it did. If she were being honest with herself, she wondered if Alistair had feelings for Brenda.

Much later, she heard the buzzer and pulled open the door. Alistair stepped forward and pulled her into his arms.

She kissed him briefly and then stepped away from him. "I didn't think that you were stopping by tonight."

His eyes narrowed. "The event was brilliant. It couldn't have gone better. But for some reason, you seem unhappy. What happened?"

She smiled at him but didn't feel the happiness she should. The event was a huge success, but somehow the negative feelings about Brenda eclipsed all of that. Maybe it was just exhaustion.

She turned away from him and walked into her living room. "I think we need a short break, Alistair. All of the changes recently have been too much."

***

He reminded himself not to react. She was hurt by his mother's unkindness. He could feel his muscles tensing and made an effort to relax his stance.

"We need to talk. Maybe you should show me the flat first?"

She crossed her arms. "There isn't much to show."

"It looks like you unpacked today."

Her mannerisms were awkward, but she led him on a brief tour that ended in the kitchen.

Her reluctance to share what was bothering her concerned him. "Do you have any wine?"

She nodded and took out the bottle that he gave away at the event.

"A good choice." He took it from her and opened it while she found wine glasses.

"I'm not sure where everything is yet."

Taking the bottle and his glass into the living area, he sat on the sofa and attempted to relax. "My mother was acting odd. I don't know what got into her. Even her apology was stilted and unconvincing. She went back to Ireland this afternoon."

Anna took a sip of wine. "I didn't need her to apologize. She made her opinion known. If anything, it may cause more resentment."

He took a sip of wine. He didn't understand his mother. "She was under false assumptions. My mother hadn't realized that Brenda and I were over. I had mentioned you a few times, but for some reason she hadn't connected the dots. She had thought I was speaking about Brenda."

Anna fidgeted with her necklace. "Clearly, she has a connection to Brenda and would much rather you were dating her."

He leaned forward. "She wants me to be happy, but she was surprised by our relationship. I can tell you that she felt horribly about how she handled all of it."

Anna said, "Something has changed between us. There's been a barrier erected, and I can't seem to get past it."

"Nothing has changed, love." Why was she acting so odd?

Her eyes were blazing and she seemed intent on starting a fight. "Maybe you're right. You're still the man who doesn't want to be fenced in and I'm still the woman who has trust issues."

Alistair placed his glass on the cocktail table. "Labels are not helpful."

Anna stood up and massaged her temples. "It's late and I have an early meeting, so I think you should go."

He stood up. "I have to fly to New York in the morning. I'll be back at the end of the week." Maybe a few days apart would help her to let go of her outrage. He couldn't control his mother or Brenda Waterman.

He pulled her into his embrace. She responded to his kiss briefly and then pulled back.

Meeting his gaze, she said, "Have a safe trip, Alistair."

He didn't want to leave her tonight, but maybe it was better than having an irrational argument. "Goodnight, Anna."

***

She held back her tears until she closed the door. Her throat tightened painfully. Why did it have to be so hard? Was it better to let him go now than to be shattered when it fell apart? Why did she feel hurt? He hadn't done anything wrong. Deciding not to overthink the situation, she forced herself to unpack a few more boxes.

When she climbed into bed exhausted, she read a text from him that said Goodnight, love.

She answered with Sleep well.

The next few days passed in a blur. Throwing herself into the daily chaos at work helped her to push aside her hurt feelings. Frances came in several times and they brainstormed how to gain new clients. The new staff that was hired was working out well, and Anna led several briefings to bring everyone together as a team.

Alistair had called during the week and asked if

she would go with him to a gala for the Wine Growers' Association on Friday evening. She agreed, but didn't stay on the phone long.

She borrowed a dress from Olivia and was ready at six o'clock. With more staffing, she had been able to have someone else cover the events that weekend.

At seven o'clock, she was beginning to get concerned. Alistair usually made it a point not to be late. She pushed away feelings of waiting as a child for her father, who rarely arrived and never on time. Being kept waiting was a trigger for her, so she pulled out her laptop and handled a few work emails.

Alistair texted and said he had been delayed in flight and could she meet him at the gala? She called the car service and headed to the event. She pushed aside her worries. It was an event, and she knew how to make small talk and keep things pleasant.

Anna recognized several people from the event she'd put together for Martin Enterprises and exchanged pleasantries with them while she kept an eye out for Alistair.

There were several promotional posters on display and she noticed that in one of them, Alistair and Brenda were standing together overlooking a vineyard.

Taking a sip of wine, she saw Brenda Waterman heading straight towards her. The woman had no boundaries.

"Has Alistair disappeared into thin air?" Her voice was high-pitched and unpleasant. She reminded Anna of an annoying mosquito, constantly buzzing around wanting to cause irritation.

Anna took a sip of wine. "His flight was

delayed."

"For your sake, I hope he wasn't delayed by one of his flight attendants. I know they service all sorts of needs en route." The model widened her eyes and feigned concern.

She couldn't believe how venomous and undignified Brenda was. "Alistair is nothing if not loyal."

Brenda glanced around the room and smiled at people lingering nearby before lowering her voice and saying, "Well… I can't believe you're hanging around waiting for a scrap of affection. Alistair is all about increasing his empire and it seems as if he no longer has an interest in your little event management company."

"Yes, we have moved on from a purely business relationship to a more personal connection." Anna kept her tone light, but refused to allow the model to push her around. She couldn't understand what drew Alistair to the hateful woman.

Brenda hesitated for a moment and said, "If you'll excuse me." Anna watched her approach another guest.

Another acquaintance came up to her and said, "Hello. I'm guessing Alistair has been delayed."

She nodded. Where was he? She needed him to rescue her.

Without any encouragement, the woman continued. "They are such a glamorous couple." Referring to the poster. "These events are not very exciting, but it reminds everyone to stay active in the association."

Anna tried to change the subject. "The wine is

delicious."

The woman openly yawned. "True. But there is nothing to do at these things."

Anna couldn't wait to escape. "Enjoy your evening."

Anna placed her glass on the nearest tray and headed for the door. She didn't need to put up with this.

A light rain was coming down so she decided to take a taxi instead of calling the car service.

Alistair was arriving when she stepped out onto the sidewalk.

He pulled her into his arms saying, "I'm sorry, love."

"It's not enough. You were late and then, by suggesting that I come here alone, you threw me to the wolves."

He stepped back and touched her cheek. "Anna."

Her emotions were ready to erupt. She had endured enough for the evening. "I'm not staying, Alistair."

His tone reminded her of someone speaking to a small child. "I promised to put in an appearance. Twenty minutes and then we can get a late dinner."

"No. This is not working for me." She couldn't make eye contact with him. "Take care of yourself, Alistair."

She signaled to the taxi driver and opened the door.

He touched her bare arm. "Let's not end the evening this way."

Climbing into the taxi, she gave the driver her address and he pulled away from the curb. Her first thought was that she let Brenda Waterman win. But she didn't want to live her life in turmoil, doubting the actions of her partner.

Alistair was brilliant, intense yet sensitive, but it wasn't enough. She needed someone she could depend on.

Letting herself into her flat, she allowed tears to slide down her cheeks. She was going to miss him desperately. In a short time, he had infiltrated all of her defenses. Why did it have to end this way?

Anna collapsed onto the sofa and sobbed. Everyone else around her knew how this would end but she had pretended otherwise. She had allowed herself to hope that their relationship would deepen and mature. But Alistair wasn't about permanence or creating a lasting bond.

Within the hour, he rang the bell to her flat. She buzzed him up but dreaded the confrontation. She wasn't ready to defend herself.

Opening the door, she stood back and invited him in. At least she had washed her face and changed out of her dress.

"I appreciate you checking on me, but I'm fine."

He roughly caught her arm. "I'm not."

She raised her voice. "I'm sorry, Alistair, but I can't live this way. I don't know if you are over Brenda or not, but I'm done with the gossip and pitiful glances."

He let go of her and stepped back. "I wanted to see you this evening. My flight was delayed and I thought it would save time if you met me there. I should have realized that it would be a setup for you."

She shook her head. "I can't trust what we had. I

know you'll disappoint me. You already have."

He spoke without any emotion. "This issue is not mine. You're carrying around baggage from your childhood. You believe that you'll be hurt or disappointed again so you shut others out before that happens. There is nothing that I can do or say that will dislodge that belief from you. You have to decide to let it go."

She could feel tears forming in her eyes. "I want to be in a relationship where I don't have to chase my partner for a scrap of attention."

He clenched his jaw. "I don't understand what has changed between us. You've been busy and have barely returned my calls."

"I'm tired of dealing with your relationship with Brenda Waterman. The woman is pure poison." She regretted her words but refused to soften her stance. Their relationship had been doomed from the start.

Alistair ran a hand through his hair. "Brenda has nothing to do with the issue between us. It's your insecurity around trusting others."

Anna wiped away a stray tear. "I don't have issues with trusting men, Alistair. Only you. You're the one who refuses to have a more meaningful relationship."

He crossed his arms. "You'd rather throw away what we have than acknowledge the truth."

She raised her voice. "I'm not wrong, Alistair. Our relationship can't survive this. We both know it."

She watched him walk out of the flat and out of her life.

She despised Brenda Waterman. But, if she were being honest, their issues were much deeper than one insufferable model. Alistair had been right. She didn't trust him. On some level, she expected him to disappoint her. It felt way too familiar to her and was right below the surface.

But what if she didn't want to live her life waiting for others to disappoint her? How could she possibly change this about herself? It was as if a dark chasm was opening up and pulling her down into the depths of murky water. She had no idea how to escape the feeling. Trying to battle the current was not working for her. Maybe she needed to give in to the hurt and sadness surrounding her. Her childhood had left deep wounds. What if she was never able to let go of the hurt that consumed her?

Chapter 12

The small commuter plane touched down in Dublin, and she hoped William remembered to pick her up at the airport. He had been distracted with work when she had called him.

It had been three weeks since she had seen Alistair. Their breakup weighed on her every day. She had been unfair to him. Holding on to resentment and past hurts instead of trusting in their relationship hadn't served her. Alistair had been right. He would never be able to fix her father abandoning her. She needed to find her own peace around it and not allow it to poison her adult relationships.

Catching sight of William, she relaxed. She needed her brother right now. He understood her without her having to say too much.

He gave her a tight hug. "So it's true?"

She looked at him, "What's true?"

"He broke your heart."

She nodded. "Can we go back to your place?"

William guided her through the crowd and into a waiting taxi.

"Don't you have a car?"

He stretched out his legs. "Yes, but it's easier to take a taxi to the airport."

Anna reached into her handbag and put on her sunglasses. "Dublin seems to suit you."

"I'm much happier living away from New York and London. Dublin is manageable."

Her brother could be an enigma. "Doesn't Diane refuse to travel here?"

"Yes. My mother does refuse, so there is that added benefit."

Anna laughed. "I know she can be impossible, but she loves you."

He nodded. She was looking forward to escaping her life for the weekend and seeing where he lived. He had taken on an old historic pub that needed a massive renovation.

William gave her a leisurely tour of the estate and then ordered in Thai food.

He opened two bottles of Guinness and took her outside to the slate patio.

"You've done a magnificent job with the renovations so far."

"I don't know what it is about this place. I like the large, open spaces, yet it is close to the city. Maybe my soul connects to the old pub that was here for years."

"Alistair would love this place."

William tilted his head to the side. "He's a great guy. Why did he break it off?"

Anna stood up and began pacing. "He didn't exactly. I did. I didn't trust him and there was this model in the background that couldn't wait to swoop in and pick up the pieces."

He raised his eyebrows. "So… you were jealous and became angry?"

Anna faced him and tried to explain. "I don't know. It was like a barrier got erected between us and I couldn't tear it down."

William took a swallow of his ale and asked, "He refused to discuss the issue?"

Anna picked up her Guinness and took a swallow. "No. He wanted to talk about it, but I couldn't. It reminded me for some reason of how Oliver treated me and I didn't want that."

He gave her a perplexed look. "I'm not following you, sis. You didn't want to speak with Alistair about your feelings of being abandoned?"

William must know that their father had neglected her. "No. I want to leave it in the past. But the truth is that I wasn't important to him. I waited forever for Oliver to come back. I ended up not seeing him for eight years. By the time I did, I was so angry with him that I couldn't let my guard down." She placed her bottle on the table and turned away.

His voice remained neutral. "Childhood memories are difficult. You weren't an adult so there is no way you would be able to understand the circumstances."

She turned and looked at him. "I'd like to think that none of it affects me, but that isn't true."

William stood. "I know Oliver tried to negotiate with your mother for years and she refused to allow any contact with you. I imagine when he told both your mother and mine about the deception that he had little choice at that point, but thought that something could be worked out."

She crossed her arms. "My mother said he had no interest in me." Was it possible that her mother lied to

215

her?

William finished his bottle. "That's your mother's bitterness talking. Ask Fionn. He found all of the correspondence after our father's death. Oliver repeatedly begged your mother for visitation and even diverted money from his company to pay her off so he could see you. Fionn had attorneys deal with all of that."

Could that have been true? Had her father tried to see her? "How could my mother possibly benefit from keeping my father away from me?"

William moved away from the table and leaned against a stone wall surrounding the patio. "She wanted to make him pay for choosing my mother over her. But it was far more complicated. He was married to Diane and she was part of his company. My mother wasn't easy to deal with. Both women were put in an impossible situation."

"It's sad, really. He caused so much heartache with his deceptive behavior." Anna looked out to the garden.

William gently turned her back towards him. "It had nothing to do with you or me. Oliver loved us and wanted to be a part of our lives. His judgment and decision-making was questionable. The odd thing was that he chose women who were strong-willed and vengeful. He must have liked the challenge."

Anna tried to put the pieces together. "So you think Oliver sought visitation and my mother blocked him?"

"I know for a fact he did. The legal documents show he sought partial custody. He was dealing with another country and your mother was blackmailing him. She accused him of taking money that belonged to his investors. I don't know how she knew that. But she was willing to go to the authorities if he didn't do what she wanted."

Why would her mother have done such a thing? Didn't she care about her daughter's happiness at all? "My life growing up would have been so different if I had known you and knew that my father cared about me."

William nodded. "It wasn't so simple. It wasn't just your mother. Diane had no interest in Oliver seeing either you or Olivia. She would have made your life miserable. He would have had to see you in London."

Why did her father lie to everyone? "It's complicated, but at least I know that he wanted to see me."

William held up his hands. "How could you doubt that?"

At least her brother knew that both of his parents had loved him. "I had a lonely childhood. After he left when I was eight, my mother became even more angry and bitter. I thought he didn't want to have anything to do with us." Anna wiped a stray tear from her face.

"Did your mother tell you that he had another family?"

She shook her head. "No. I found out when his death was reported in the London papers. I sent a message to Olivia through her social media."

He looked off into the distance. "I'm sorry that you didn't get a chance to know him when you were an adult. He was kindhearted and fun. He had his flaws, but he also made the world a better place."

William hugged her. "I miss him."

She hugged him back briefly and then he went inside to get another Guinness for each of them.

Sitting back down at the table, Anna said, "When I was sixteen, he came to my school and sat down next to me on a bench. I was so surprised that I said nothing. He asked how I was and gave me his business card. He said if I ever needed anything that I could call him. I kept the card, but I never called him. I guess I thought he would always be around."

William held her gaze. "Your mother prevented you from going to the funeral?"

She nodded. She was seventeen and under her mother's control. She grieved his loss even though she wasn't able to attend his funeral.

"Maybe you should visit his gravesite. It might give you some closure. He wouldn't want you to hang on to your sadness. If he could do everything over, I believe he would make different choices."

Anna looked at her brother. "Yes, but one of us might not be here if that were the case."

William touched his bottle to hers and said, "To us and not being afraid to live."

They spent the rest of the weekend visiting sites in Dublin and then William brought her back to the airport.

He hugged her tight in the terminal and said, "Find a way to make your dreams come true and don't let anything stand in the way of your happiness."

"I love you." She kissed his cheek.

"Me too. Safe trip."

***

Several days later, Anna decided to drive out and

visit her father's gravesite with flowers. Her aunt and uncle were away, so Olivia explained how to find the small, private cemetery.

Eight years ago, her mother had insisted that she not attend the funeral. Anna had asked Olivia about the day and her sister had shared each memory in detail.

Walking up to the small chapel, Anna could almost see those who had gathered for the funeral. She had seen photographs in the media that were etched in her memory.

The last vivid memory she had of her father, she was eight years old and he was leaving. Her parents had fought and she had been in the back garden trying to escape the anger and rage between them. She heard the door slam and then his car start. Peering through the slotted fence, she saw him look back at the house and then drive away.

As an adult she realized that, in the heat of the moment, he had no idea he would never return. His leaving had to do with her mother and deciding to return to his other life. It was an impossible choice. Knowing her mother, she would never have allowed visitation or meetings. Once he left, he would have been completely cut off.

She now understood that, given the opportunity, Oliver would have maintained a connection with her. He had provided for them and given her mother a house and a settlement. But, the best gift he had given Anna was Olivia and William. She couldn't imagine her life without them.

Walking to her father's gravesite, she placed the lilies in front of the stone marker. Kneeling down, she said, "I forgive you. I know you would have made different choices if you were able. I love you, Dad. I'll always love you."

She remembered being sixteen and sitting briefly on the bench with him. It had been a strange encounter. By that point, she had figured out how to hold in her emotions and not allow herself to feel them. Had she been able to express her emotions that day, she would have told him how hurt and sad she had been. She would have explained how much she missed his presence in her life.

At eighteen, she had decided to begin using the Bolles name and had pursued a relationship with each of her siblings. She was proud to be part of the Bolles family even though it was difficult at times.

Anna walked back to her rented car and a memory of Oliver surfaced. He had taken her to the National Gallery when she was six or seven years old. Her mother must have been doing something else, because they had the entire day together. He had held her hand and answered any question she asked. He had taken her out to lunch and asked her what she wanted to be when she grew up. He had encouraged her to work hard in mathematics, told her that she had come from a long line of relatives that were gifted with numbers. Was it possible that he knew then that he would leave them?

Tears spilled down her face. Mostly for the little girl that had to give up her father.

Getting back in the car, she no longer felt angry or hurt. Instead, Anna realized she was in control of her future. She could choose whether or not to forgive him or her mother. She could hold on to bitterness or let it go. It wasn't a difficult choice. She needed to be free of the burden so she could seek her own path to happiness.

Chapter 13

On the first Friday in early December, Anna forced herself out of bed and pulled on her running clothes. She didn't want to brave the cold weather, but she methodically tightened her sneakers and put on a hat, gloves, and vest. Tucking a key into the pocket in her waistband, she stepped outside in the cold and began a slow warm-up towards the park.

She breathed in the cold air and tried to clear her mind of thoughts about Alistair. She needed time to grieve for her lost childhood and acknowledge her emotional pain. She couldn't move forward until she was willing to face how she felt about all of it and understand how it shaped her beliefs about the world.

Spotting a man in a business suit step out of a hotel, she slowed her pace. The way he drew his coat together against the wind was instantly familiar to her. The number of times an image of Alistair popped into her head was unbelievable. She reminded herself to push forward and let go of her desire to reach out to him. Her pace remained constant throughout the park until finally she had to slow down and walk home. Her breathes were coming in short gasps and she no longer felt the cold.

Anna stepped into the flat, closing the door and

listening to the silence. She didn't want to live her life this way. She missed Alistair. She missed him with a craving so deep that she collapsed against the door and slid to the floor. Tears ran down her face and she gave into the feeling of falling into a dark chasm. She created the distance between them. A thought emerged that she had the power to fix the damage that she had caused.

After taking a shower, she picked up her phone and called Martin Enterprises. Alistair's assistant told her that he had been in New York but had returned home yesterday. She had been sending him updates on Gala & More, but he hadn't responded. If she could find a way to see him, maybe she could explain why she had difficulty trusting others.

She needed to take the weekend off and seek out Alistair. Texting Elyse and Frances, she begged them to cover her events. Her phone dinged within seconds with a response from Frances that it wouldn't be a problem. Elyse texted her be brave.

The last argument replayed over and over in her head, and it had become clear to her that she had been unfair to him. Pushing away the worry and anxiety, she called the car service and got dressed. Even seeing a glimpse of him was worth the emotional turmoil. Dressing in jeans and a black cashmere jumper, she pulled her hair back into a ponytail and applied a small amount of makeup to cover the dark circles under her eyes.

The trip out to his house seemed endless. What if he wasn't home or not willing to see her? She glanced out the window at the snow covering the rolling hills. In London, there was barely any trace of snow left, but out in the country everything gleamed white and pristine.

The driver had the radio on low and she listened to a Christmas song. At Gala & More they had been planning holiday events for weeks and had organized many parties, but with each one, she sank deeper into her private loneliness and kept herself in survival mode.

When his estate pulled into view, her breath stilled in her chest. He would send her away. She had waited too long to come and see him.

Stopping in front of his house, the driver got out and opened her door. For a moment, she contemplated asking him to take her back to London. But instead, she made herself get out of the car and thank him. The older man tipped his hat to her when she handed him a twenty-pound note and returned to the driver's seat.

The estate had been decorated with white lights and a large wreath on the front door. She walked up the path and rang the bell. Helen, his housekeeper, answered the door and brought her into the formal living room, saying that she would let Alistair know that he had a guest. The fireplace was roaring, the tree decorated, and there were flowers everywhere. Maybe he wasn't alone.

Her nerves made her feel ill and she took a deep breath and reminded herself not to lose hope. It had been several minutes since the housekeeper left in search of Alistair. Maybe he was refusing to see her? She couldn't sit still and got up to stand in front of the fire. She took in another deep breath and tried to calm her nerves.

She heard the front door open and turned as

Alistair walked in. He held her gaze but didn't say anything.

Her arms wrapped around her waist. "Alistair."

He came into the room fully and unbuttoned his coat. "Is there a problem?"

She bit her lip and then looked away from him. "I wanted to see you. I've missed you."

He took off his coat and flung it on a nearby chair. "You've missed a man incapable of having a long-term relationship?" Her harsh words must have stayed with him.

She met his gaze and held her stomach, trying to hold back the anxiety and nauseous feeling. "I shouldn't have said those hurtful things to you."

"What changed your mind?"

Her voice cracked. "I don't know."

"You'll have to do better than that." He stepped away from her. "Sit. I'll ask Helen to bring tea."

He was going to send her away. Every hard angle of his body told her that he would never forgive her. It was a mistake coming to see him. He didn't want her in his life.

She picked up her coat and bag. She couldn't stay and listen to him end things. Fumbling with the front door, Anna didn't hear him come up behind her.

He roughly pulled her around to face him. "Instead of facing this, you're going to leave?"

She didn't try and stop the tears from falling. "I can't. It's too much."

He held her against the massive door. "If you are not willing to fight for us, there is nothing I can do."

His warmth infiltrated her body and she said, "I am willing to fight for us, but I can't ask more of you

225

than you are willing to give."

He tightened his grip on her arms. "You've asked nothing of me. What do you want?"

She said without thinking, "I want you to love me."

He closed the gap between them and his mouth covered hers. After kissing her, he pulled back and wiped the tears from her face.

"I love you, Anna Bolles. I have for a long time."

She pulled him close and rested her head on his chest. She worried that her legs would give out, but he held her against his body, then brought her back into the living room and sat with her on the sofa.

The housekeeper arrived with a tray of tea and placed it on a side table before leaving the room.

Anna got up and sat on his lap. "I've missed you so much. My heart has been breaking a little more each day we have been apart."

"Mine, too." He kissed her gently and wiped the tears from her cheeks.

The housekeeper called out, "I'm going to my sister's. See you tomorrow."

Anna clutched his shirt. "Why didn't you come and find me?"

He gently stroked her back. "I didn't think you were ready to let go of the past."

Looking into his eyes, she said, "I was probably ready within hours of you walking out, but it took a while to gather the courage to come and see you."

He held her gaze and her heart felt like it was melting. "Does this mean that you'll move in?"

She threw her arms around him and kissed his neck. "Yes. Whatever you want."

He held her tight. "I never got the chance to tell you that you did a remarkable job with the event. My sales team recorded huge numbers the next day."

She said quietly, "I can't even think about that night."

Alistair tightened his embrace. "My mother was wrong and feels horrible. I was telling her in the weeks that led up to the event that I was in love and planned to propose that night. She had thought I was talking about Brenda Waterman. I can't imagine why she would. She must have been so enmeshed in her own life and couldn't see the truth."

Tears slid down her face. "It was my fault. I was so willing to believe that you didn't care about me and would seek out an affair. I should have had more faith in you."

His voice was soft. "Please don't cry. We both had a part to play. I should have explained myself more fully and made allowances for your fears."

Anna took in a deep breath. "I've needed to make peace with the past. I realized that if I couldn't, then it would continue to overshadow my happiness. I've forgiven my parents for being so selfish and I'm ready to let my insecurities go."

He brushed a strand of hair from her face. "That must have been difficult. I've had to face some of my own issues around disappointment and commitment."

She couldn't believe he was opening up to her so fully. "What do you mean?"

"I've had some heart-to-heart conversations with my mother. Her odd behavior towards you allowed me to confront old resentments. She can be controlling and I've protected her, but I let her know that something had shifted within me."

"I hope I didn't cause an issue between you and her." It was endearing that he cared so much about his mother.

"It was time. She's proud of the man I became and encouraged my independence, but she wanted to control my emotional life. I hadn't recognized it before. But when I told her that I intended to pursue you even if that made her upset, something shifted. I was no longer worried about being trapped by someone else's expectations."

She gently stroked his hair. "How did your mother handle that?"

His arms around her tightened. "She threw a fit and accused me of being like my father. She went through an entire gamut of emotions. At times accusatory, threatening, tearful—until she realized I was not going to be swayed. She began to let her guard down, and shared with me that she was afraid of losing me. We were able to discuss the reasons why she hid her pregnancy from my father for years and the choices she made."

Anna chewed on her lower lip. "How are things now?"

He met her gaze. "They're a bit strained, but at least the conversation isn't superficial. It's real. It's allowed me to face certain things about my father and the reasons why I wanted to remain free."

Anna looked up at the ceiling. "It's crazy how much work we both needed to do."

He ran his hand down her back. "We have complicated backgrounds, but somehow finding you helped heal me in a way I would have never predicted."

She kissed his jawline and then his neck.

"I can't believe you're here." Alistair repositioned her, standing briefly to place her on the sofa and stretching out next to her.

Kissing her provocatively, he pulled off her sweater and began to explore her body fully.

She had missed him so much. She couldn't believe she was in his arms, and kissed him back with all of her love and desire for him.

***

Later that evening, he insisted that they get out of bed and go in search of food.

She pulled on his t-shirt, he put on a pair of briefs, and they headed downstairs to the kitchen.

He drew her into a tight embrace. "You've gotten too thin, love."

"It's crazy how a broken heart will do that, but I'm ready to devour anything."

The housekeeper had left a casserole that he put into the oven. He pulled out different cheeses, some bread, and fruit.

Anna sat on one of the stools. "Did you know that I would come back to you?"

Alistair stopped assembling the meal. "It depended on the day. Some days, I was convinced you would come to me. But some days I began to doubt that you would and I began to plot how I could win you back."

He walked towards her and she said, "I had to work out a few things. It was hard. I spoke with my brother and then visited my father's gravesite. I didn't realize how much my father leaving had affected me."

Stopping next to her, he tucked a strand of hair behind her ear. "If you had let it go much longer, I would have come."

"I love you." She smiled at him. The words came so easily. Why couldn't she say them before?

He met her gaze. "I hope you keep on loving me forever." Alistair kissed her and said, "Give me one moment." Then he disappeared from the kitchen.

She let out the breath she had been holding.

He walked back in and stood in front of her. "I love you, Anna. This may not be the most romantic location, but I can't wait any longer."

Her hand went to her belly to try and ease the fluttering in her stomach.

He looked down into her eyes and said, "Will you marry me?"

Alistair opened the box he had retrieved, and she saw a beautifully set diamond and sapphire engagement ring.

Anna gasped and tears began to fall freely. He loved her and wanted to marry her. All she could manage was an emphatic nod. He pulled her into a devouring kiss.

Much later, Alistair put the ring on her finger and they sat in a candlelit dining room and had dinner.

She glanced at the ring. "I need to call Olivia."

He laughed. "Can you wait and we can visit them tomorrow? Your nieces will be overjoyed to be part of a wedding."

After they cleared the plates, they sat together on the sofa watching the fire.

Anna enjoyed listening to his stories about the winery and his grandparents. She couldn't wait to meet them again and begin to get to know them. Even the idea of meeting his mother again didn't worry her.

Anna turned towards him. "The vineyard would be the perfect place for the wedding."

He smiled at her. "It's a good thing you're an extraordinary event planner."

She curled up next to him on the sofa. "Olivia told me years ago that she had a design in mind for a wedding gown."

"You are lucky to have both a sister and a brother."

She put thoughts of the wedding out of her mind and relished knowing that she and Alistair would spend their life together. She had missed him every moment of every day.

Watching Alistair add a log to the fire, Anna couldn't believe love had found her. Even though she had done everything wrong, somehow everything worked out.

Acknowledgments

It takes a team working together to take a manuscript and produce a compelling novel. I have several people to thank for their hard work, dedication and encouragement along this journey. Getting the story to the reader makes the entire struggle worth it!

To **Erica Monroe**, your powerful feedback and willingness to delve into the fray helped me see things in a much different way. I'll forever be grateful for your kind words of wisdom while insisting that I could 'dig deeper'. You have the discerning quality to not only see someone's strengths and weaknesses but to know how to communicate it to them. I've become a much better writer for it.

To **Stephanie Kay**, your smart critiques and encouragement helped me to keep going. I can't thank you enough for reading this novel twice and catching all sorts of omissions and errors.

To **Meghan Hogue**, your editing skills and insight helped turn this story into a polished novel. It's been wonderful to work with a professional who can see the bigger picture yet fix the small problems.

To **Kim Killion**, your creative genius in cover design and overall professionalism make you an absolute pleasure to work with. Thank you for another amazing cover!

To **Christina Tetreault**, your steadfast loyalty and support made me believe that I could succeed as a writer. Even on the hardest days, I could reach out to you for assistance. Your knowledge and expertise in self-publishing is second to none. I hope we share many more writing adventures together.

To the **members of RWA**, including all of the writers who have joyously shared their craft, I can't thank you enough for sharing your ideas, inspiration and words of wisdom. I'd like to particularly thank **Bob Mayer, Kristan Higgins, Virginia Kantra and Angela James** for their amazing workshops.

To **my children**, for always being proud of me and trying not to interrupt too many times.

To **my husband**, **David**, for your endless support and your eagerness to tell people that you are the inspiration behind the ideas.

And to **my readers**, thank you for taking a chance on this novel. I hope you enjoy it immensely!

Thank You for Reading

Thank you so much for reading ***The Secret Heiress***! I hope you enjoyed the story. It would be amazing if you could take a few minutes to review this book on Amazon – your feedback is quite valuable.

Stay in Touch

I love to hear from readers and answer every email personally. Please visit my website, www.susiewarren.com, to sign up for my newsletter and a chance to read my next book early, receive information on discounted prices and free books!

The Next Book in this Series:

The Chosen Heir

From enemies to lovers…

William Bolles is a charming risk-taker who hides his sentimental streak behind an uncompromising business intellect. When his sister pleads with him to save a garment manufacturer and insists Bridget is the perfect candidate to help salvage the operation, he remembers a charged past meeting with Bridget. But he decides to play along and brings Bridget into the fold, more for the challenge of proving her wrong until complications and disagreements muddy the water.

Bridget North is a beautiful, hard-working marketing whiz with an extraordinary fashion sense. She pursues the truth, even if it becomes difficult or challenging. Raised by dreamers in a chaotic environment, she vowed to create order and stability in her life. Until one evening she breaks her own rules and allows herself to be drawn into an emotional exchange with William Bolles.

William is everything she's said she never wants. She should stay away from him, yet she can't deny the scorching passion between them…